BUNNY vs. MONKEY

-BOOK THREE-

BY JAMIE SMART

YEAR TWO
JANUARY-JUNE

d b FICKLING
David Fickling Books

the PHOENIX

SCHOLASTIC

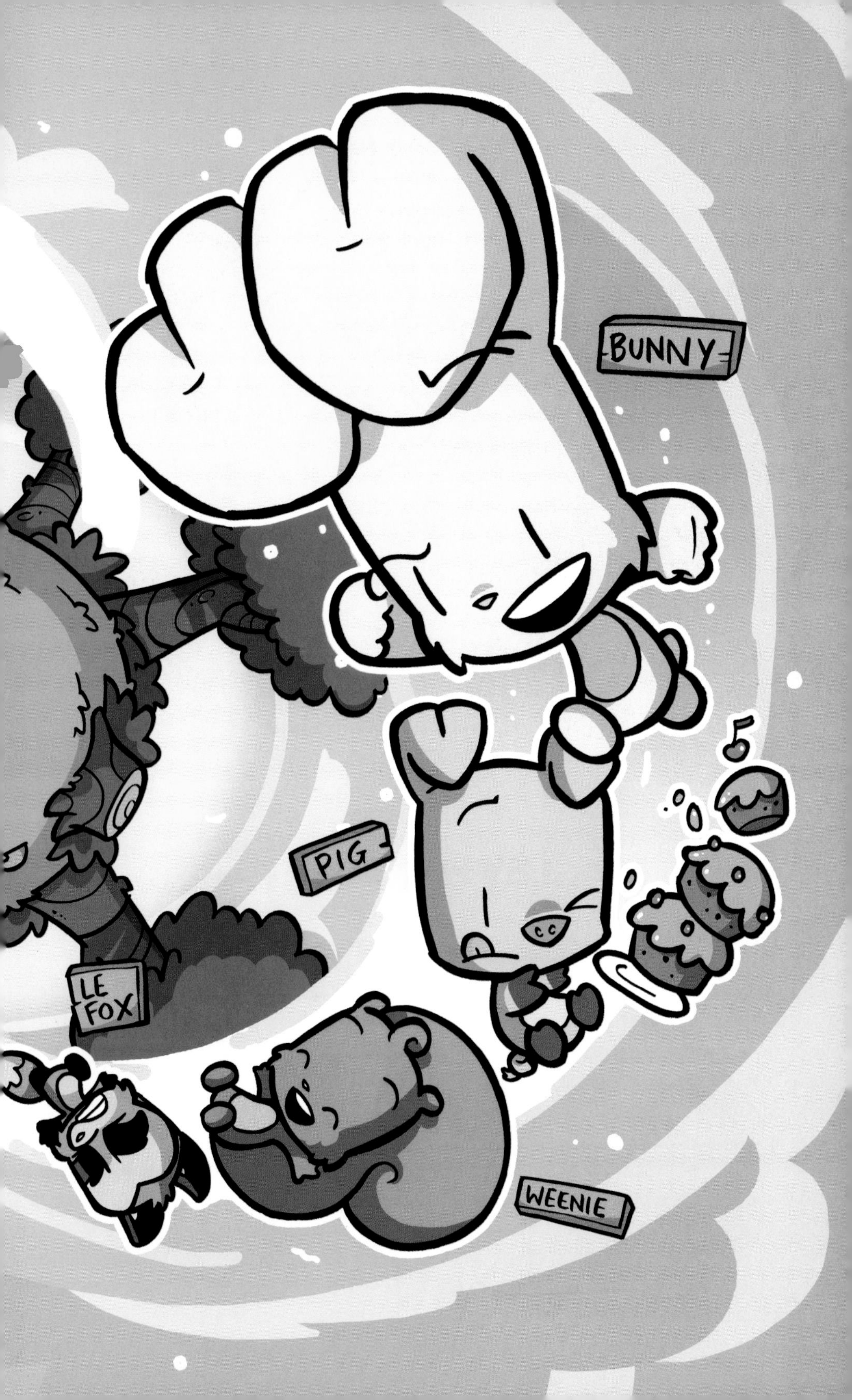

BUNNY
PIG
LE FOX
WEENIE

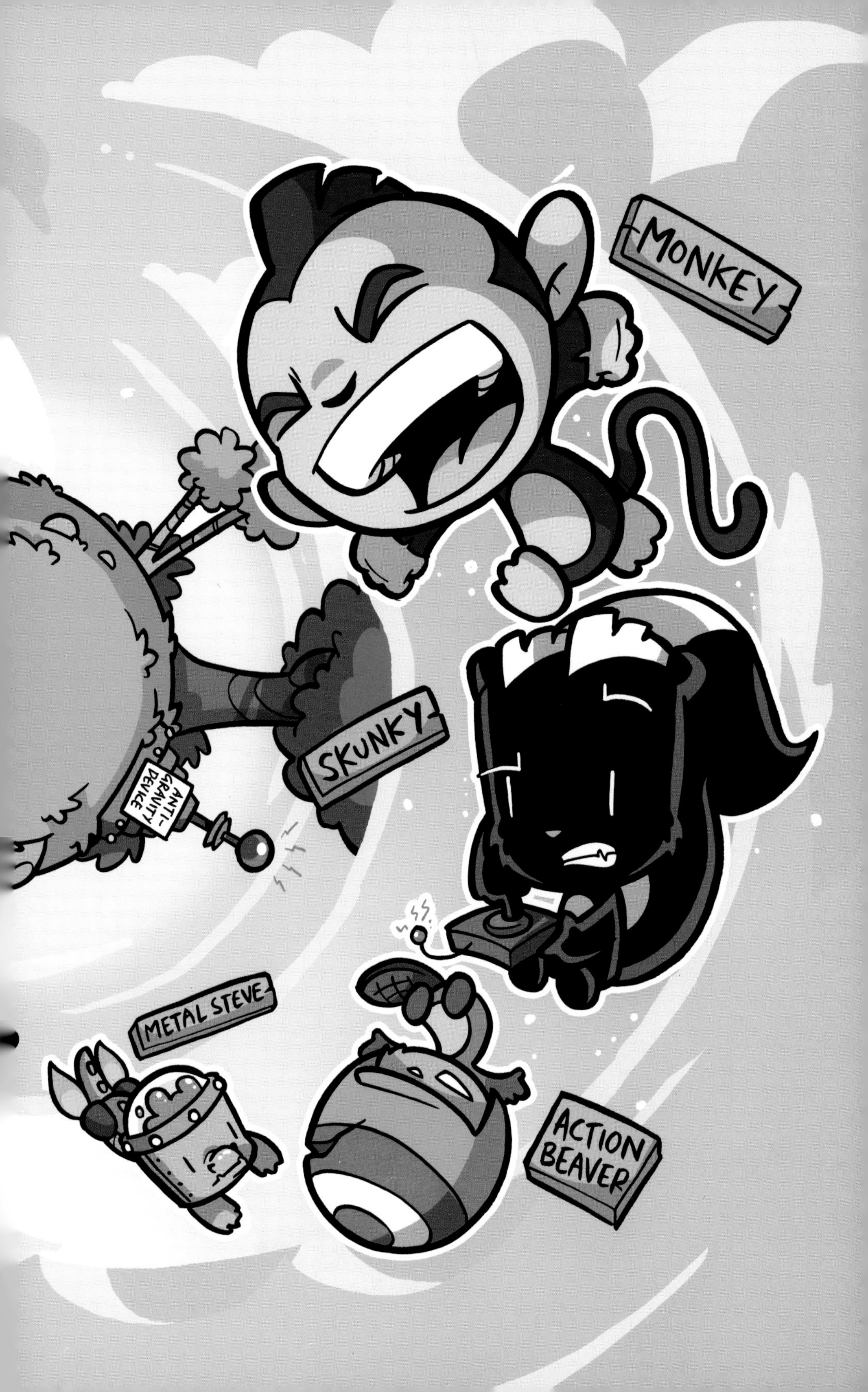
MONKEY
SKUNKY
ANTI-GRAVITY DEVICE
METAL STEVE
ACTION BEAVER

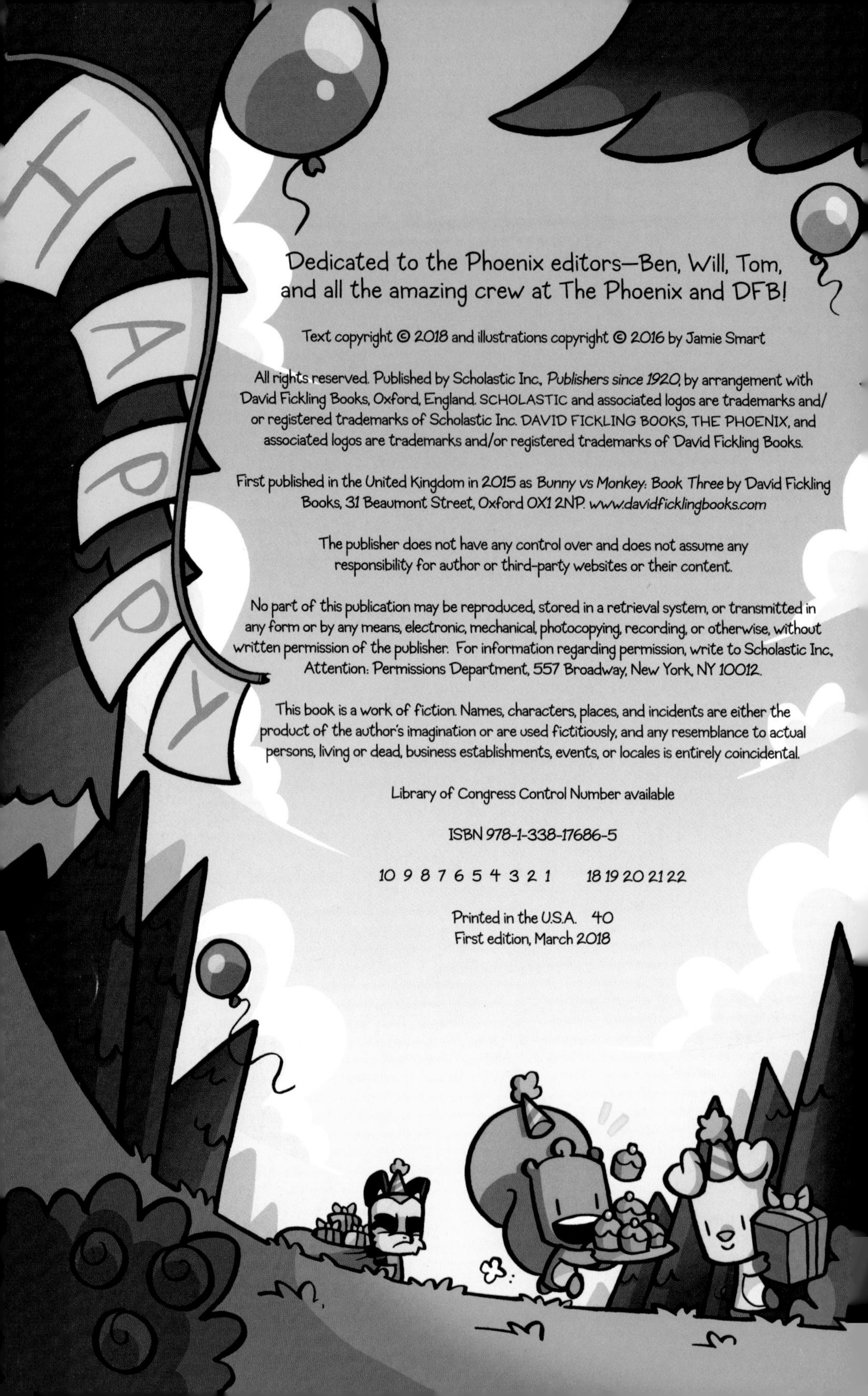
HAPPY

Dedicated to the Phoenix editors—Ben, Will, Tom, and all the amazing crew at The Phoenix and DFB!

First published in the United Kingdom in 2015 as *Bunny vs Monkey: Book Three* by David Fickling Books, 31 Beaumont Street, Oxford OX1 2NP. *www.davidficklingbooks.com*

Library of Congress Control Number available

ISBN 978-1-338-17686-5

10 9 8 7 6 5 4 3 2 1 18 19 20 21 22

Printed in the U.S.A. 40
First edition, March 2018

THE CONTENTS!

JANUARY! ✿ ✿ ✿
PAGE 6 - "LOG OFF!"
PAGE 8 - "LIONEL"
PAGE 10 - "CA-MOO-FLARJ!"
PAGE 12 - "THE QUEST FOR
BLACKBEARD'S TREASURE!"

FEBRUARY!
PAGE 14 - "T3-DDY"
PAGE 16 - "WHAT LIES
      BENEATH!"
PAGE 20 - "CASA DEL PIG!"
PAGE 22 - "MEET RANDOLPH!"

MARCH!
PAGE 24 - "THE STENCH!"
PAGE 26 - "THE EDUCATING OF MISTER
      METAL STEVE!"
PAGE 28 - "FISHYPLOPS!"
PAGE 30 - "BAD CROWD!"
PAGE 32 - "THE BIGGEST, MOSTEST
ENORMOUSEST EXPLOSION IN THE WORLD!"

APRIL! ❀ ❀ ❀
PAGE 34 - "BILLION-DOLLAR
BEAVER!"
PAGE 36 - "THE KAKAPO
POO KABOOM!"
PAGE 38 - "MONKEY
BUTLER!"

MAY! + + + +
PAGE 40 - "THE BIG EYE AM!"
PAGE 42 - "ON THE ROAD!"
PAGE 44 - "THE PURPLE!"
PAGE 46 - "THE WEIRD,
WEIRD WOODS!
(PART ONE)"

JUNE!
PAGE 48 - "THE WEIRD, WEIRD WOODS!
(PART TWO)"
PAGE 50 - "BUNNYOPIA!"
PAGE 52 - "OCTO-FOX!"
PAGE 54 - "WEENIE'S BIG ADVENTURE!"
PAGE 56 - "BRAIN-ACHE!"
PAGE 58 - "WOODLAND STORY!"
PAGE 60 - "SO MANY MONKEYS!"

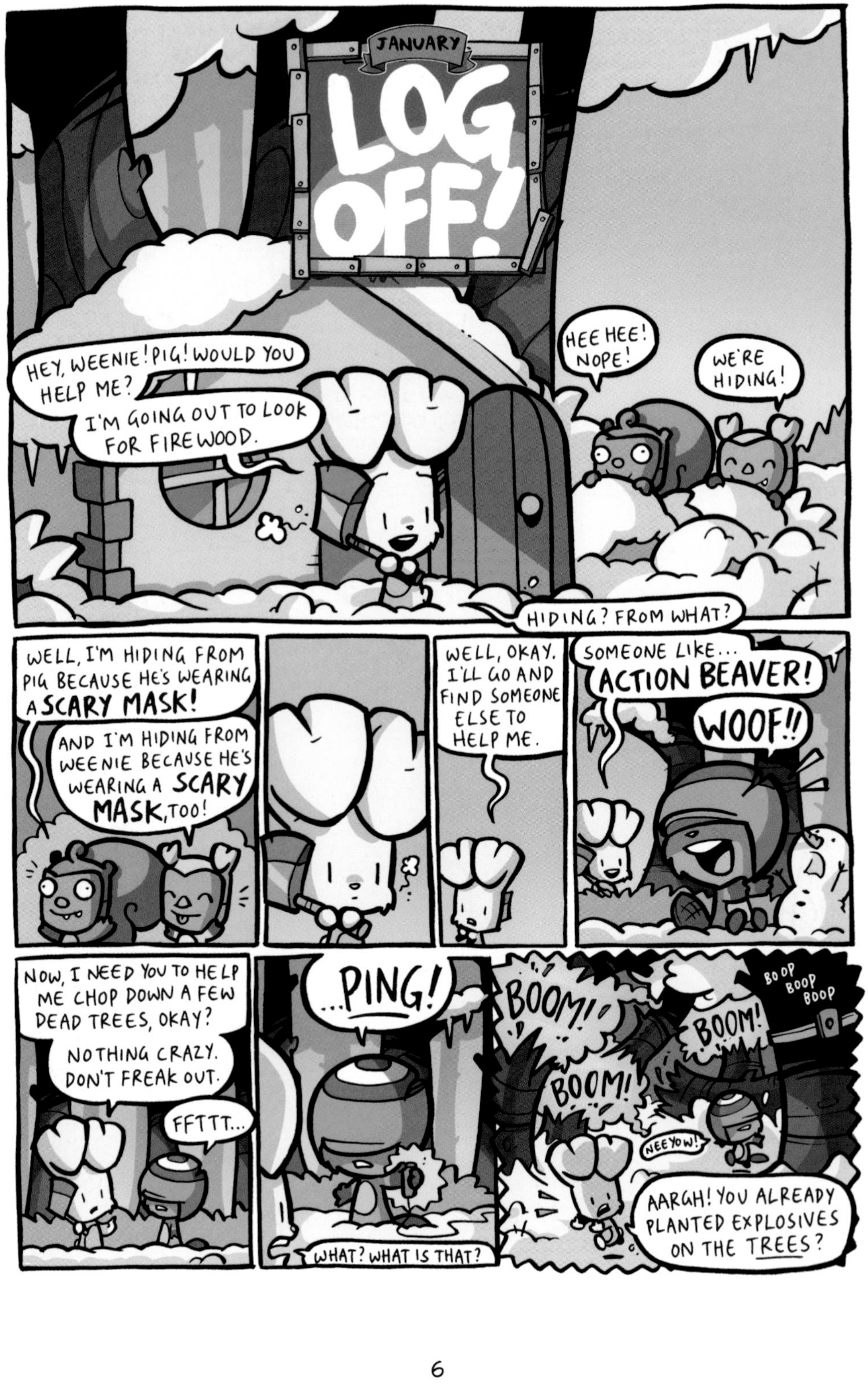
JANUARY
LOG OFF!
HEY, WEENIE! PIG! WOULD YOU HELP ME?
I'M GOING OUT TO LOOK FOR FIREWOOD.
HEE HEE! NOPE!
WE'RE HIDING!
HIDING? FROM WHAT?
WELL, I'M HIDING FROM PIG BECAUSE HE'S WEARING A SCARY MASK!
AND I'M HIDING FROM WEENIE BECAUSE HE'S WEARING A SCARY MASK, TOO!
WELL, OKAY. I'LL GO AND FIND SOMEONE ELSE TO HELP ME.
SOMEONE LIKE... ACTION BEAVER!
WOOF!!
NOW, I NEED YOU TO HELP ME CHOP DOWN A FEW DEAD TREES, OKAY?
NOTHING CRAZY. DON'T FREAK OUT.
FFTTT...
...PING!
WHAT? WHAT IS THAT?
BOOM!
BOOP BOOP BOOP
BOOM!
BOOM!
NEEYOW!
AARGH! YOU ALREADY PLANTED EXPLOSIVES ON THE TREES?

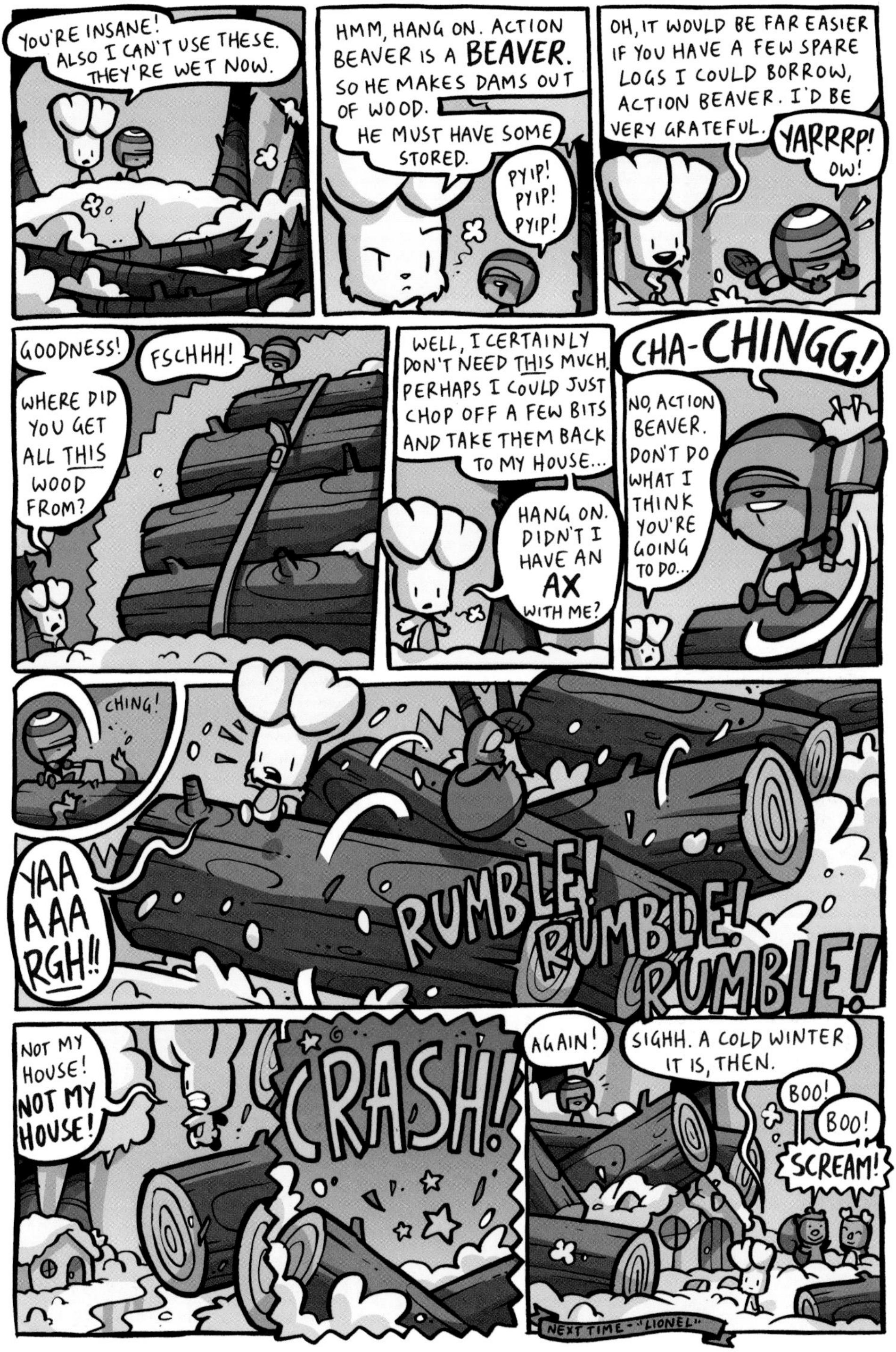
YOU'RE INSANE! ALSO I CAN'T USE THESE. THEY'RE WET NOW.
HMM, HANG ON. ACTION BEAVER IS A BEAVER. SO HE MAKES DAMS OUT OF WOOD.
HE MUST HAVE SOME STORED.
PYIP! PYIP! PYIP!
OH, IT WOULD BE FAR EASIER IF YOU HAVE A FEW SPARE LOGS I COULD BORROW, ACTION BEAVER. I'D BE VERY GRATEFUL.
YARRRP! OW!
GOODNESS!
FSCHHH!
WHERE DID YOU GET ALL THIS WOOD FROM?
WELL, I CERTAINLY DON'T NEED THIS MUCH. PERHAPS I COULD JUST CHOP OFF A FEW BITS AND TAKE THEM BACK TO MY HOUSE...
HANG ON. DIDN'T I HAVE AN AX WITH ME?
CHA-CHINGG!
NO, ACTION BEAVER. DON'T DO WHAT I THINK YOU'RE GOING TO DO...
CHING!
YAAAAARGH!!
RUMBLE! RUMBLE! RUMBLE!
NOT MY HOUSE! NOT MY HOUSE!
CRASH!
AGAIN!
SIGHH. A COLD WINTER IT IS, THEN.
BOO!
BOO!
SCREAM!
NEXT TIME - "LIONEL"

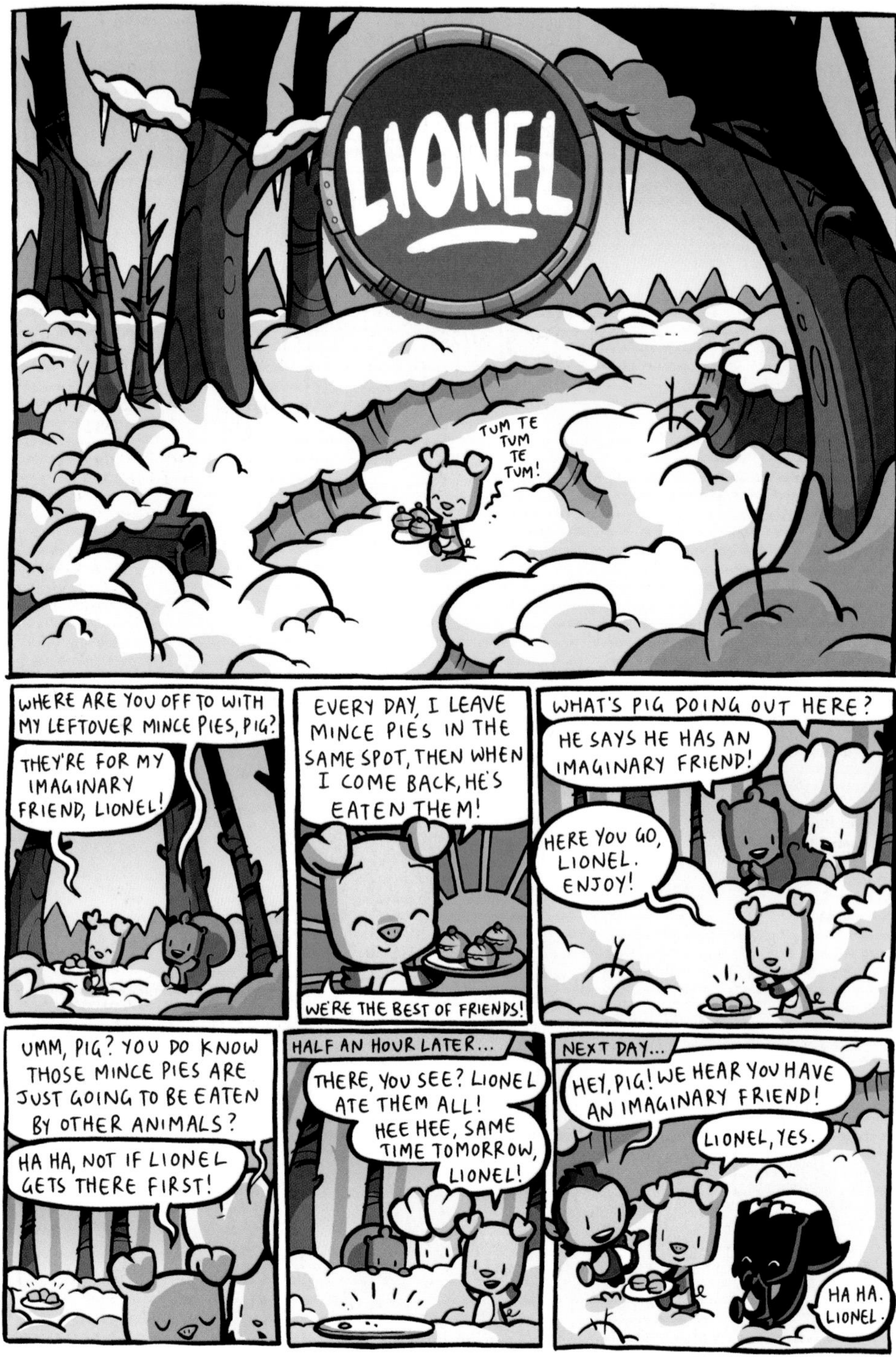
LIONEL
TUM TE TUM TE TUM!
WHERE ARE YOU OFF TO WITH MY LEFTOVER MINCE PIES, PIG?
THEY'RE FOR MY IMAGINARY FRIEND, LIONEL!
EVERY DAY, I LEAVE MINCE PIES IN THE SAME SPOT, THEN WHEN I COME BACK, HE'S EATEN THEM!
WE'RE THE BEST OF FRIENDS!
WHAT'S PIG DOING OUT HERE?
HE SAYS HE HAS AN IMAGINARY FRIEND!
HERE YOU GO, LIONEL. ENJOY!
UMM, PIG? YOU DO KNOW THOSE MINCE PIES ARE JUST GOING TO BE EATEN BY OTHER ANIMALS?
HA HA, NOT IF LIONEL GETS THERE FIRST!
HALF AN HOUR LATER...
THERE, YOU SEE? LIONEL ATE THEM ALL!
HEE HEE, SAME TIME TOMORROW, LIONEL!
NEXT DAY...
HEY, PIG! WE HEAR YOU HAVE AN IMAGINARY FRIEND!
LIONEL, YES.
HA HA. LIONEL.

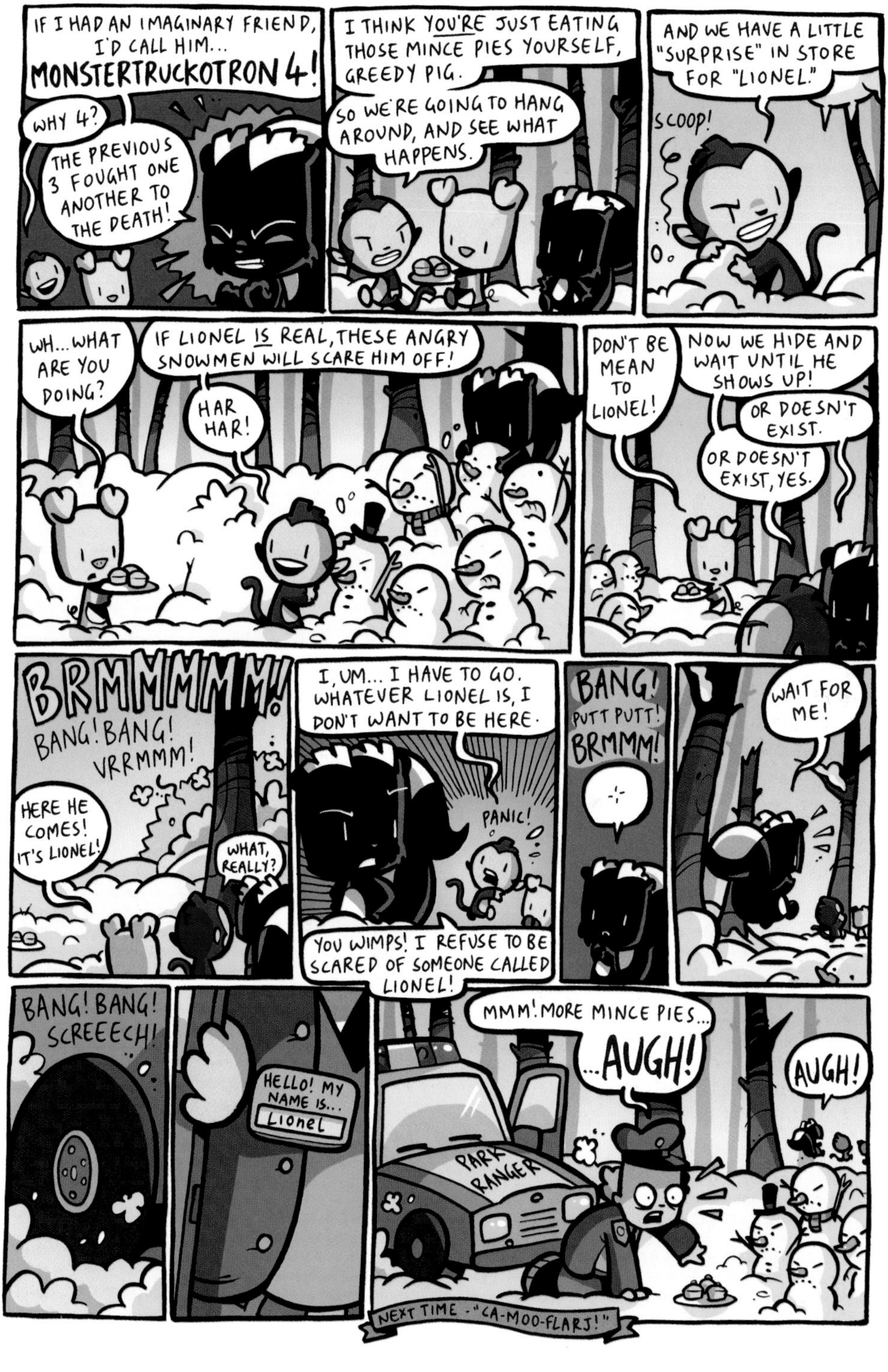
IF I HAD AN IMAGINARY FRIEND, I'D CALL HIM... MONSTERTRUCKOTRON 4!
WHY 4?
THE PREVIOUS 3 FOUGHT ONE ANOTHER TO THE DEATH!
I THINK YOU'RE JUST EATING THOSE MINCE PIES YOURSELF, GREEDY PIG.
SO WE'RE GOING TO HANG AROUND, AND SEE WHAT HAPPENS.
AND WE HAVE A LITTLE "SURPRISE" IN STORE FOR "LIONEL."
SCOOP!
WH... WHAT ARE YOU DOING?
IF LIONEL IS REAL, THESE ANGRY SNOWMEN WILL SCARE HIM OFF!
HAR HAR!
DON'T BE MEAN TO LIONEL!
NOW WE HIDE AND WAIT UNTIL HE SHOWS UP!
OR DOESN'T EXIST.
OR DOESN'T EXIST, YES.
BRMMMMM!
BANG! BANG! VRRMMM!
HERE HE COMES! IT'S LIONEL!
WHAT, REALLY?
I, UM... I HAVE TO GO. WHATEVER LIONEL IS, I DON'T WANT TO BE HERE.
PANIC!
YOU WIMPS! I REFUSE TO BE SCARED OF SOMEONE CALLED LIONEL!
BANG! PUTT PUTT! BRMMM!
WAIT FOR ME!
BANG! BANG! SCREEECH!
HELLO! MY NAME IS... Lionel
PARK RANGER
MMM! MORE MINCE PIES... ...AUGH!
AUGH!
NEXT TIME - "CA-MOO-FLARJ!"

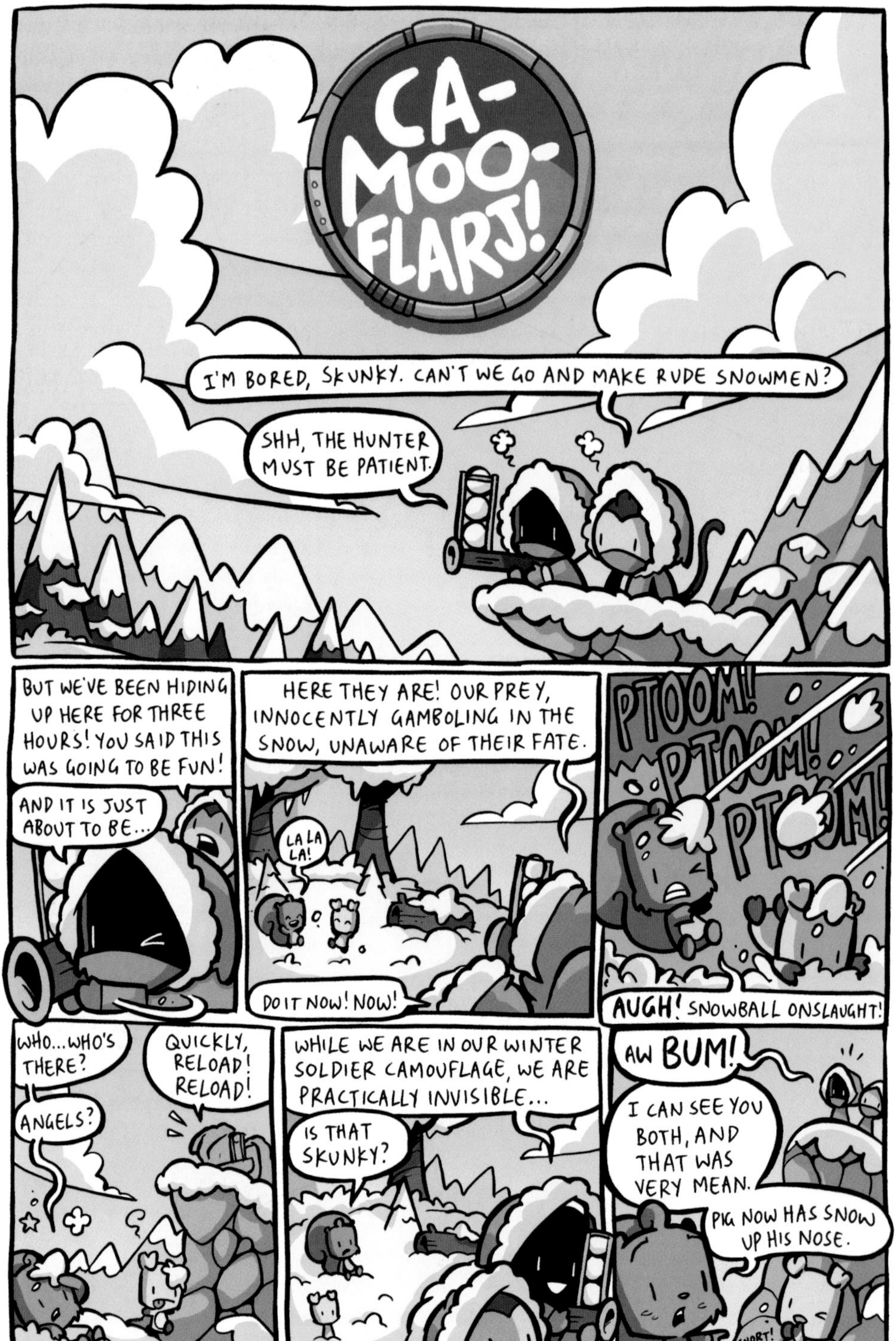
CA-MOO-FLARJ!
I'M BORED, SKUNKY. CAN'T WE GO AND MAKE RUDE SNOWMEN?
SHH, THE HUNTER MUST BE PATIENT.
BUT WE'VE BEEN HIDING UP HERE FOR THREE HOURS! YOU SAID THIS WAS GOING TO BE FUN!
AND IT IS JUST ABOUT TO BE...
HERE THEY ARE! OUR PREY, INNOCENTLY GAMBOLING IN THE SNOW, UNAWARE OF THEIR FATE.
LA LA LA!
DO IT NOW! NOW!
PTOOM! PTOOM! PTOOM!
AUGH! SNOWBALL ONSLAUGHT!
WHO...WHO'S THERE?
ANGELS?
QUICKLY, RELOAD! RELOAD!
WHILE WE ARE IN OUR WINTER SOLDIER CAMOUFLAGE, WE ARE PRACTICALLY INVISIBLE...
IS THAT SKUNKY?
AW BUM!
I CAN SEE YOU BOTH, AND THAT WAS VERY MEAN.
PIG NOW HAS SNOW UP HIS NOSE.
SNORT!

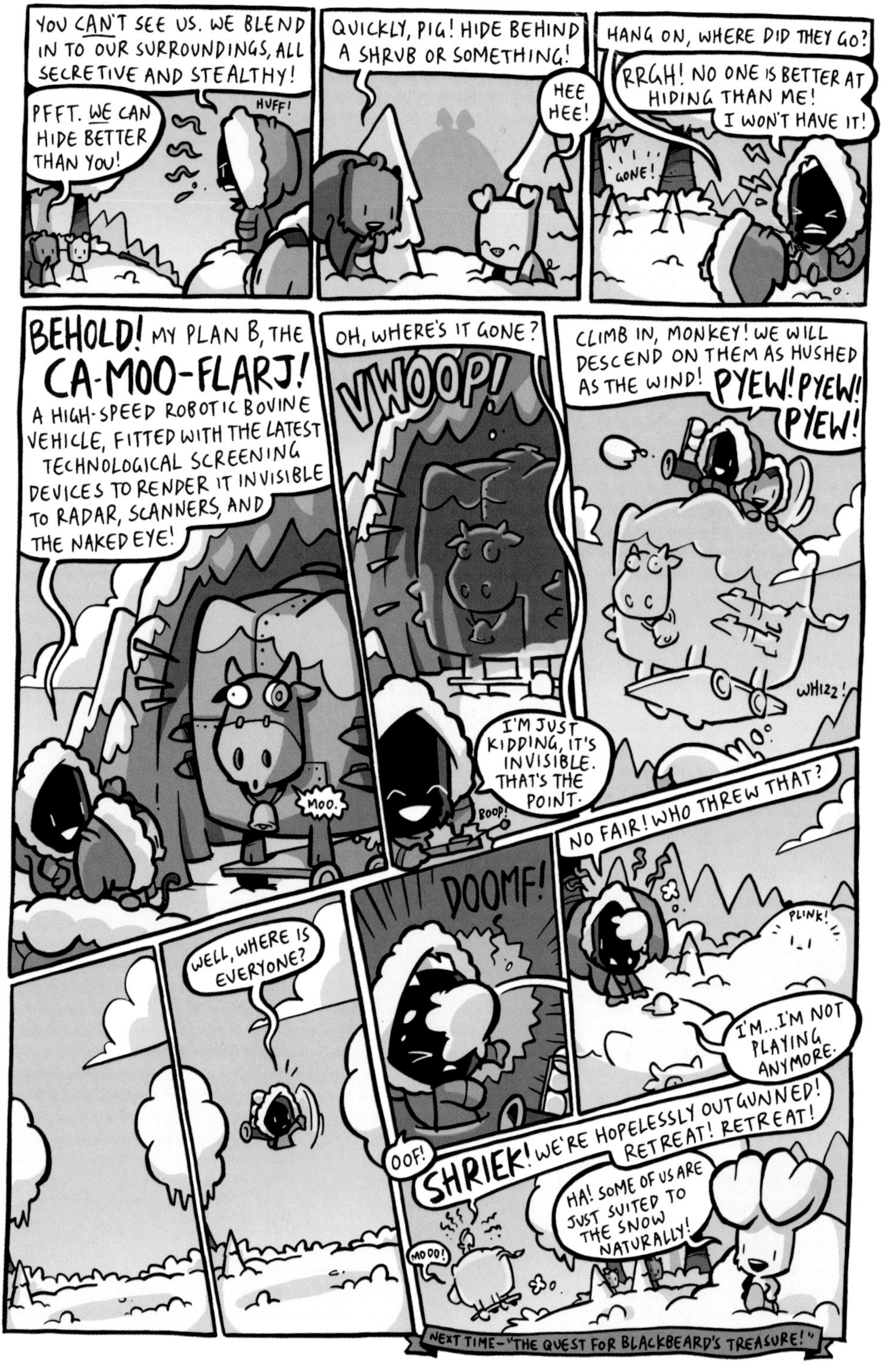
YOU CAN'T SEE US. WE BLEND IN TO OUR SURROUNDINGS, ALL SECRETIVE AND STEALTHY!
PFFT. WE CAN HIDE BETTER THAN YOU!
HUFF!
QUICKLY, PIG! HIDE BEHIND A SHRUB OR SOMETHING!
HEE HEE!
HANG ON, WHERE DID THEY GO?
GONE!
RRGH! NO ONE IS BETTER AT HIDING THAN ME! I WON'T HAVE IT!
BEHOLD! MY PLAN B, THE CA-MOO-FLARJ! A HIGH-SPEED ROBOTIC BOVINE VEHICLE, FITTED WITH THE LATEST TECHNOLOGICAL SCREENING DEVICES TO RENDER IT INVISIBLE TO RADAR, SCANNERS, AND THE NAKED EYE!
MOO.
OH, WHERE'S IT GONE?
VWOOP!
I'M JUST KIDDING, IT'S INVISIBLE. THAT'S THE POINT.
BOOP!
CLIMB IN, MONKEY! WE WILL DESCEND ON THEM AS HUSHED AS THE WIND!
PYEW! PYEW! PYEW!
WHIZZ!
MOO
NO FAIR! WHO THREW THAT?
PLINK!
I'M...I'M NOT PLAYING ANYMORE.
WELL, WHERE IS EVERYONE?
DOOMF!
OOF!
SHRIEK! WE'RE HOPELESSLY OUTGUNNED! RETREAT! RETREAT!
HA! SOME OF US ARE JUST SUITED TO THE SNOW NATURALLY!
MOOO!
NEXT TIME—"THE QUEST FOR BLACKBEARD'S TREASURE!"

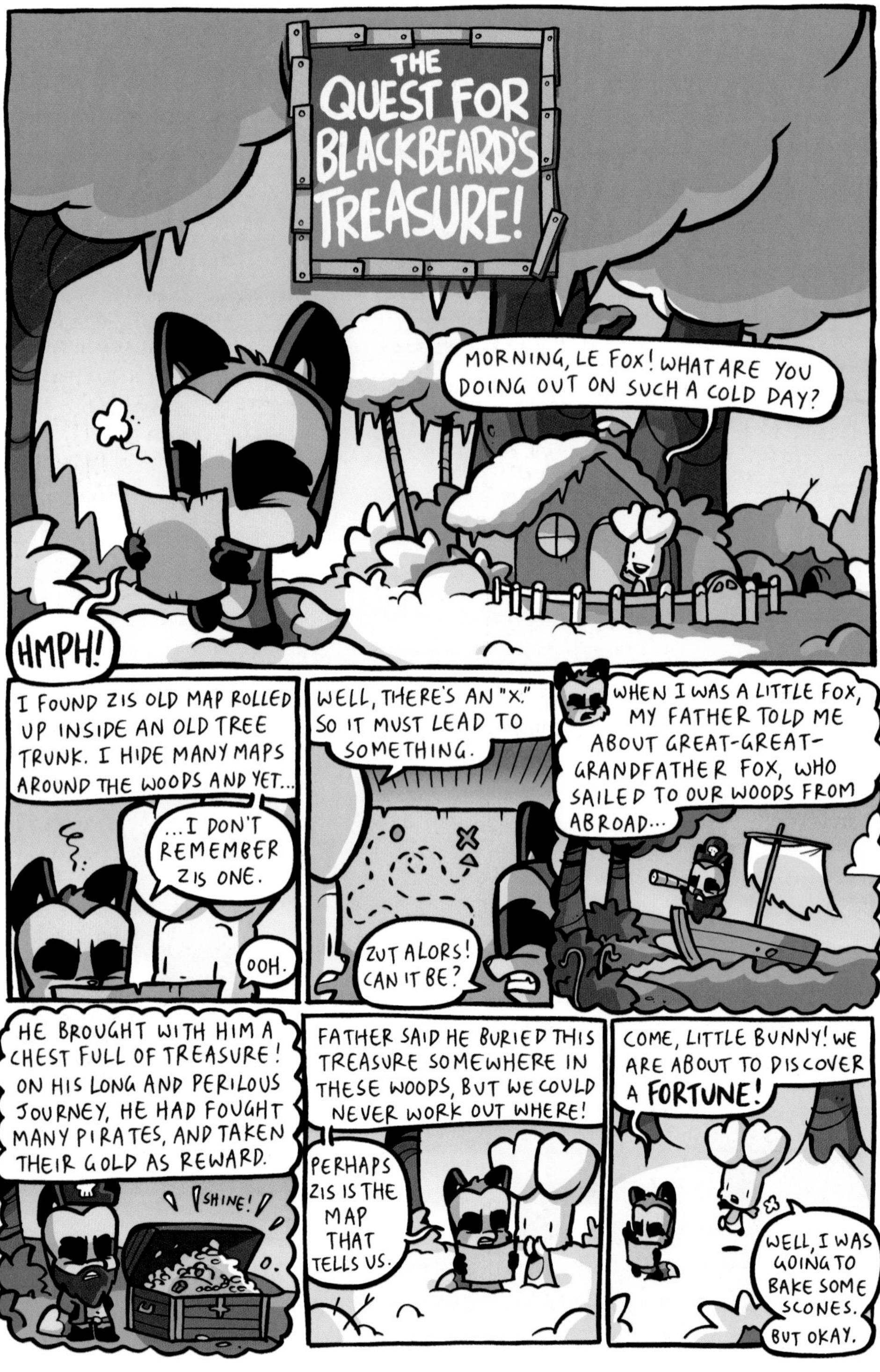
THE QUEST FOR BLACKBEARD'S TREASURE!
MORNING, LE FOX! WHAT ARE YOU DOING OUT ON SUCH A COLD DAY?
HMPH!
I FOUND ZIS OLD MAP ROLLED UP INSIDE AN OLD TREE TRUNK. I HIDE MANY MAPS AROUND THE WOODS AND YET...
...I DON'T REMEMBER ZIS ONE.
OOH.
WELL, THERE'S AN "X." SO IT MUST LEAD TO SOMETHING.
ZUT ALORS! CAN IT BE?
WHEN I WAS A LITTLE FOX, MY FATHER TOLD ME ABOUT GREAT-GREAT-GRANDFATHER FOX, WHO SAILED TO OUR WOODS FROM ABROAD...
HE BROUGHT WITH HIM A CHEST FULL OF TREASURE! ON HIS LONG AND PERILOUS JOURNEY, HE HAD FOUGHT MANY PIRATES, AND TAKEN THEIR GOLD AS REWARD.
SHINE!
FATHER SAID HE BURIED THIS TREASURE SOMEWHERE IN THESE WOODS, BUT WE COULD NEVER WORK OUT WHERE!
PERHAPS ZIS IS THE MAP THAT TELLS US.
COME, LITTLE BUNNY! WE ARE ABOUT TO DISCOVER A **FORTUNE!**
WELL, I WAS GOING TO BAKE SOME SCONES.
BUT OKAY.

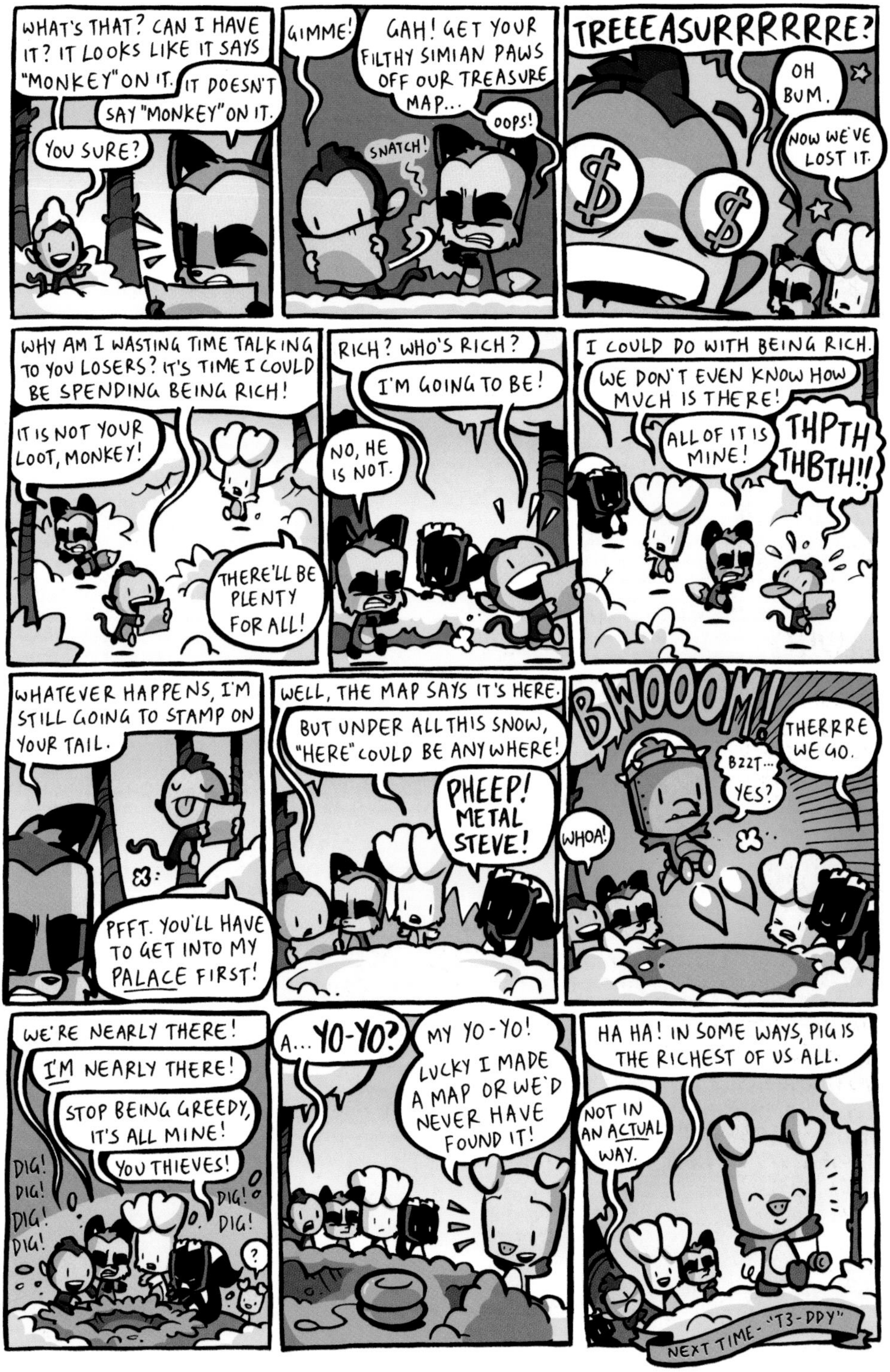
WHAT'S THAT? CAN I HAVE IT? IT LOOKS LIKE IT SAYS "MONKEY" ON IT.
IT DOESN'T SAY "MONKEY" ON IT.
YOU SURE?
GIMME!
GAH! GET YOUR FILTHY SIMIAN PAWS OFF OUR TREASURE MAP...
SNATCH!
OOPS!
TREEEASURRRRRRE?
OH BUM.
NOW WE'VE LOST IT.
WHY AM I WASTING TIME TALKING TO YOU LOSERS? IT'S TIME I COULD BE SPENDING BEING RICH!
IT IS NOT YOUR LOOT, MONKEY!
THERE'LL BE PLENTY FOR ALL!
RICH? WHO'S RICH?
I'M GOING TO BE!
NO, HE IS NOT.
I COULD DO WITH BEING RICH.
WE DON'T EVEN KNOW HOW MUCH IS THERE!
ALL OF IT IS MINE!
THPTH THBTH!!
WHATEVER HAPPENS, I'M STILL GOING TO STAMP ON YOUR TAIL.
PFFT. YOU'LL HAVE TO GET INTO MY PALACE FIRST!
WELL, THE MAP SAYS IT'S HERE.
BUT UNDER ALL THIS SNOW, "HERE" COULD BE ANYWHERE!
PHEEP! METAL STEVE!
BWOOOM!
THERRRE WE GO.
BZZT... YES?
WHOA!
WE'RE NEARLY THERE!
I'M NEARLY THERE!
STOP BEING GREEDY, IT'S ALL MINE!
YOU THIEVES!
DIG! DIG! DIG! DIG!
DIG! DIG!
?
A... YO-YO?
MY YO-YO!
LUCKY I MADE A MAP OR WE'D NEVER HAVE FOUND IT!
HA HA! IN SOME WAYS, PIG IS THE RICHEST OF US ALL.
NOT IN AN ACTUAL WAY.
NEXT TIME - "T3-DDY"

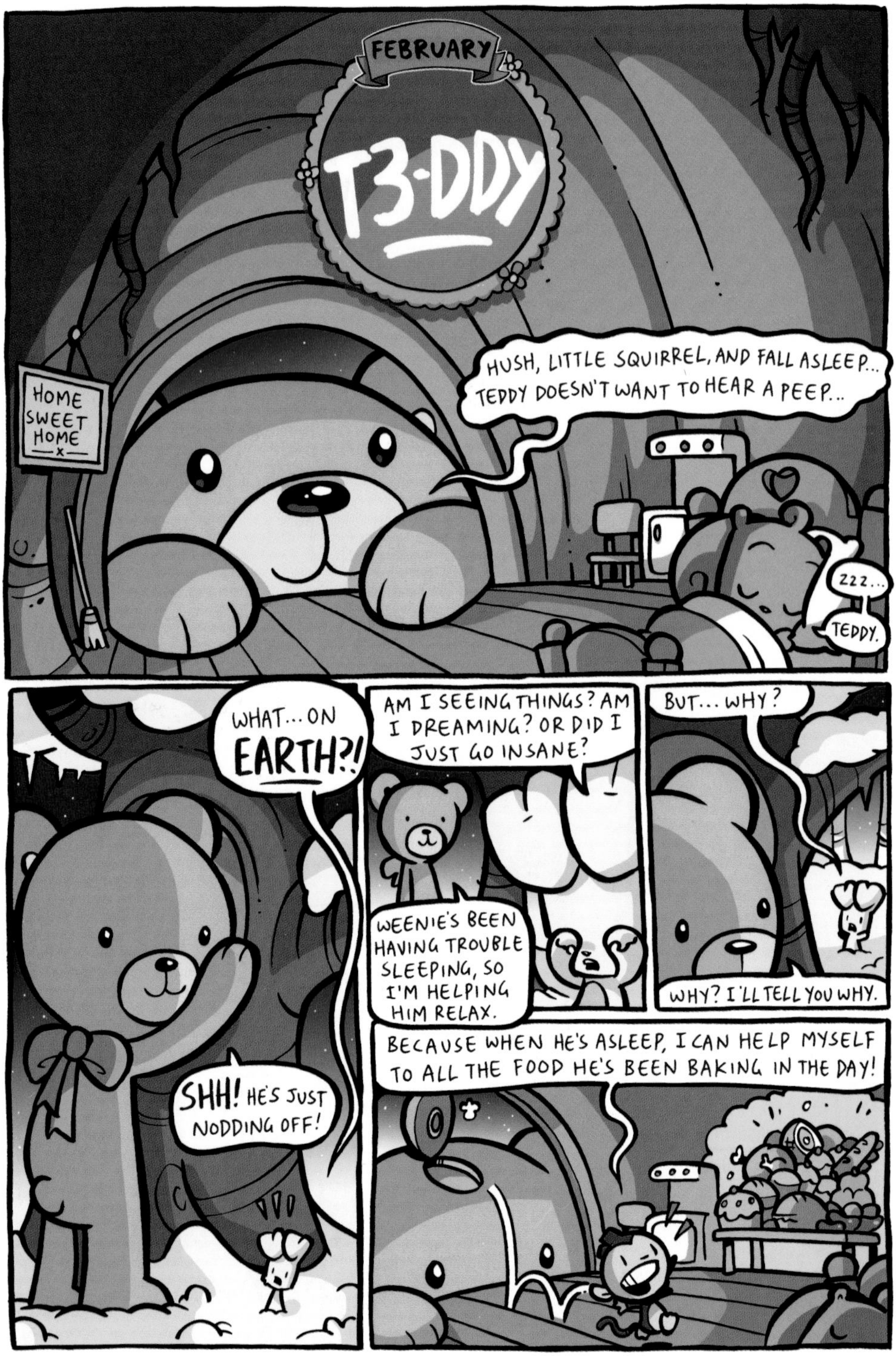
FEBRUARY
T3-DDY
HOME SWEET HOME
HUSH, LITTLE SQUIRREL, AND FALL ASLEEP... TEDDY DOESN'T WANT TO HEAR A PEEP...
ZZZ...
TEDDY.
WHAT... ON EARTH?!
SHH! HE'S JUST NODDING OFF!
AM I SEEING THINGS? AM I DREAMING? OR DID I JUST GO INSANE?
WEENIE'S BEEN HAVING TROUBLE SLEEPING, SO I'M HELPING HIM RELAX.
BUT... WHY?
WHY? I'LL TELL YOU WHY.
BECAUSE WHEN HE'S ASLEEP, I CAN HELP MYSELF TO ALL THE FOOD HE'S BEEN BAKING IN THE DAY!

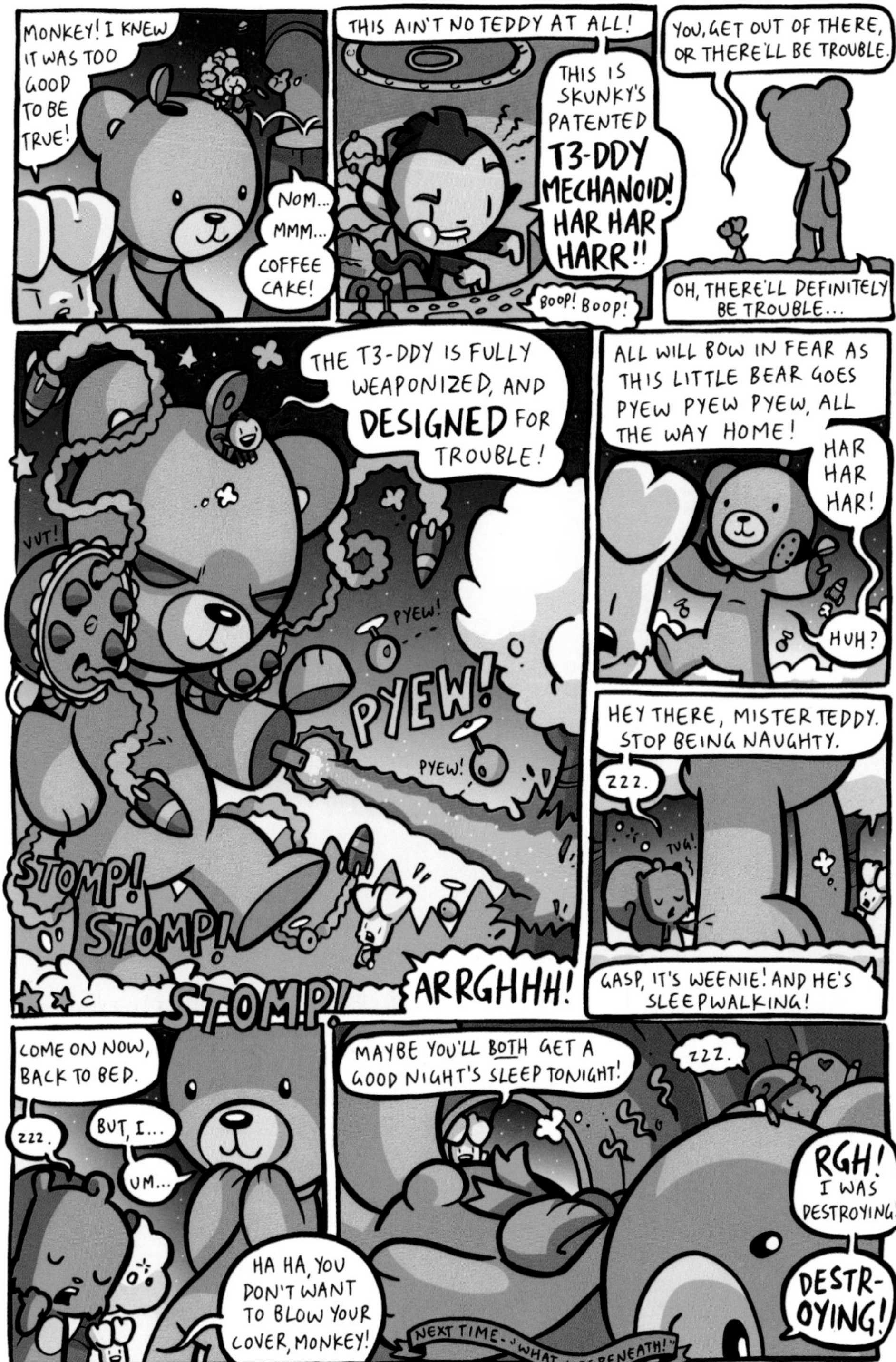
MONKEY! I KNEW IT WAS TOO GOOD TO BE TRUE!
NOM...
MMM...
COFFEE CAKE!
THIS AIN'T NO TEDDY AT ALL!
THIS IS SKUNKY'S PATENTED T3-DDY MECHANOID! HAR HAR HARR!!
BOOP! BOOP!
YOU, GET OUT OF THERE, OR THERE'LL BE TROUBLE.
OH, THERE'LL DEFINITELY BE TROUBLE...
THE T3-DDY IS FULLY WEAPONIZED, AND DESIGNED FOR TROUBLE!
VVT!
PYEW!
PYEW!
PYEW!
STOMP!
STOMP!
STOMP!
ARRGHHH!
ALL WILL BOW IN FEAR AS THIS LITTLE BEAR GOES PYEW PYEW PYEW, ALL THE WAY HOME!
HAR HAR HAR!
HUH?
HEY THERE, MISTER TEDDY. STOP BEING NAUGHTY.
ZZZ.
TUG!
GASP, IT'S WEENIE! AND HE'S SLEEPWALKING!
COME ON NOW, BACK TO BED.
ZZZ.
BUT, I...
UM...
HA HA, YOU DON'T WANT TO BLOW YOUR COVER, MONKEY!
MAYBE YOU'LL BOTH GET A GOOD NIGHT'S SLEEP TONIGHT!
ZZZ.
RGH! I WAS DESTROYING!
DESTR-OYING!
NEXT TIME - "WHAT LIES BENEATH!"

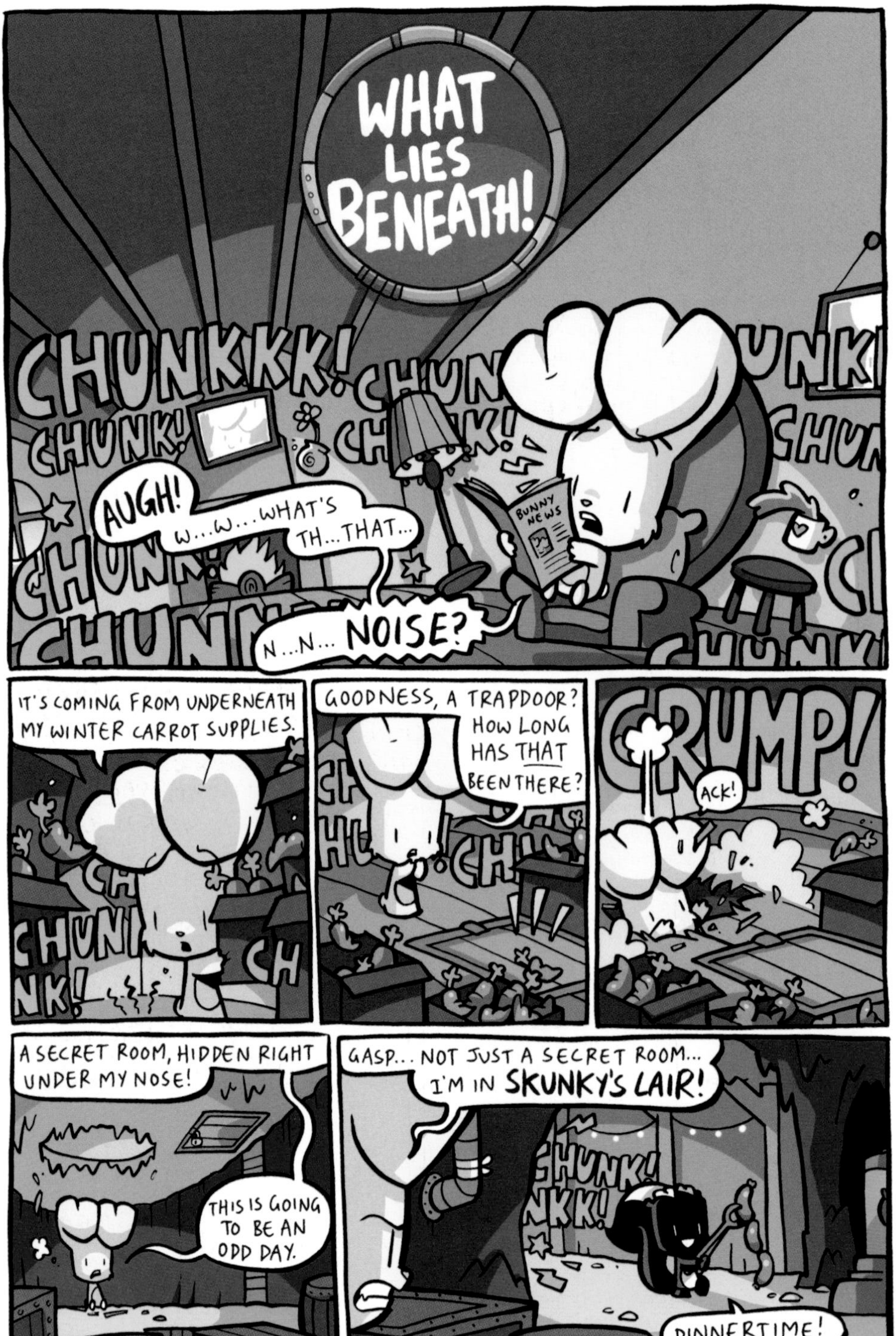
WHAT LIES BENEATH!
CHUNKKK! CHUNK! CHUNK! CHUNK!
AUGH!
W...W...WHAT'S TH...THAT...
N...N... NOISE?
BUNNY NEWS
IT'S COMING FROM UNDERNEATH MY WINTER CARROT SUPPLIES.
GOODNESS, A TRAPDOOR?
HOW LONG HAS THAT BEEN THERE?
CRUMP!
ACK!
A SECRET ROOM, HIDDEN RIGHT UNDER MY NOSE!
THIS IS GOING TO BE AN ODD DAY.
GASP... NOT JUST A SECRET ROOM... I'M IN SKUNKY'S LAIR!
DINNERTIME!

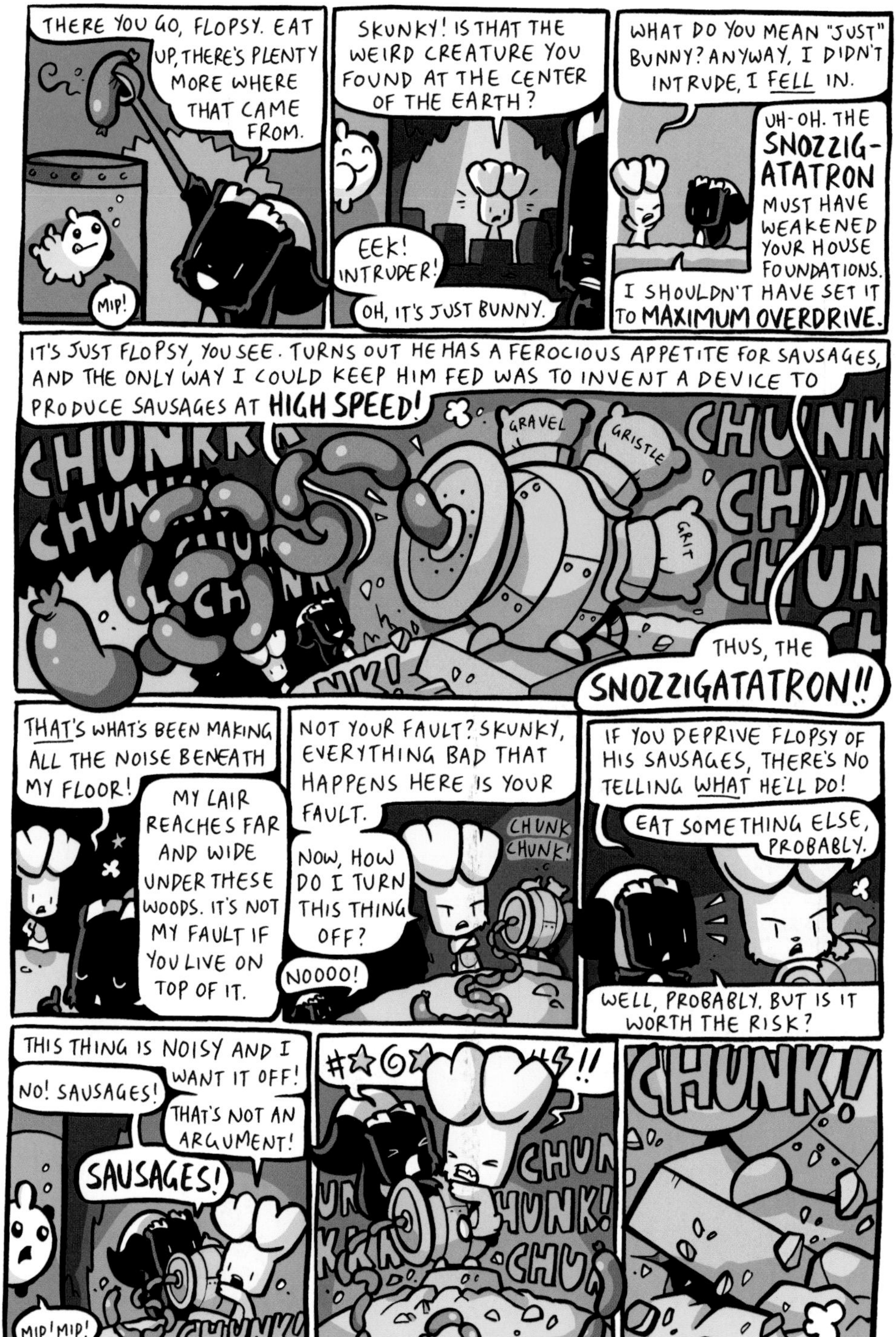
THERE YOU GO, FLOPSY. EAT UP, THERE'S PLENTY MORE WHERE THAT CAME FROM.
MIP!
SKUNKY! IS THAT THE WEIRD CREATURE YOU FOUND AT THE CENTER OF THE EARTH?
EEK! INTRUDER!
OH, IT'S JUST BUNNY.
WHAT DO YOU MEAN "JUST" BUNNY? ANYWAY, I DIDN'T INTRUDE, I FELL IN.
UH-OH. THE SNOZZIGATATRON MUST HAVE WEAKENED YOUR HOUSE FOUNDATIONS. I SHOULDN'T HAVE SET IT TO MAXIMUM OVERDRIVE.
IT'S JUST FLOPSY, YOU SEE. TURNS OUT HE HAS A FEROCIOUS APPETITE FOR SAUSAGES, AND THE ONLY WAY I COULD KEEP HIM FED WAS TO INVENT A DEVICE TO PRODUCE SAUSAGES AT HIGH SPEED!
GRAVEL
GRISTLE
GRIT
THUS, THE SNOZZIGATATRON!!
THAT'S WHAT'S BEEN MAKING ALL THE NOISE BENEATH MY FLOOR!
MY LAIR REACHES FAR AND WIDE UNDER THESE WOODS. IT'S NOT MY FAULT IF YOU LIVE ON TOP OF IT.
NOT YOUR FAULT? SKUNKY, EVERYTHING BAD THAT HAPPENS HERE IS YOUR FAULT.
CHUNK CHUNK!
NOW, HOW DO I TURN THIS THING OFF?
NOOOO!
IF YOU DEPRIVE FLOPSY OF HIS SAUSAGES, THERE'S NO TELLING WHAT HE'LL DO!
EAT SOMETHING ELSE, PROBABLY.
WELL, PROBABLY. BUT IS IT WORTH THE RISK?
THIS THING IS NOISY AND I WANT IT OFF!
NO! SAUSAGES!
THAT'S NOT AN ARGUMENT!
SAUSAGES!
MIP! MIP!
CHUNK!
CHUNK!

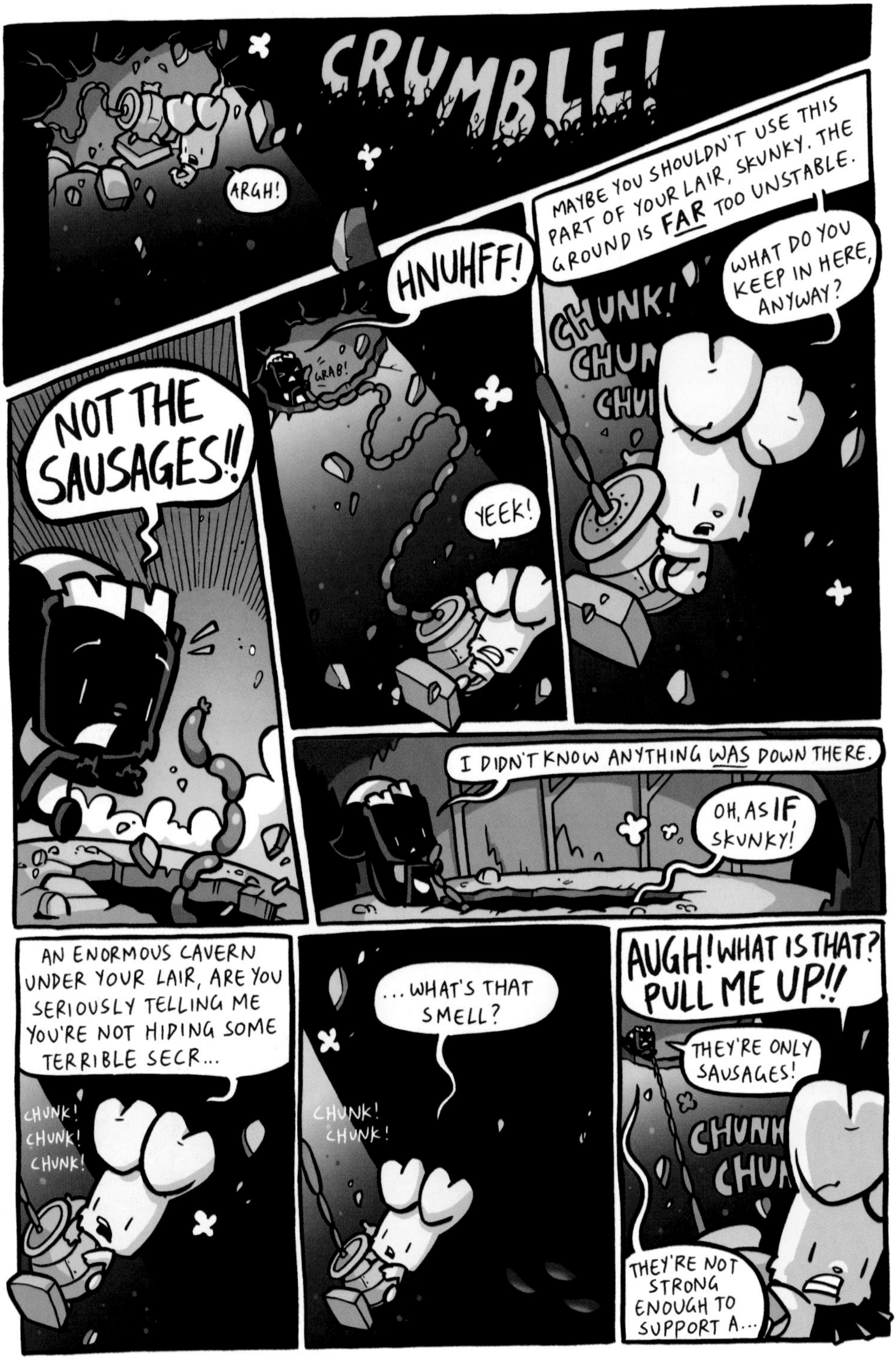
CRUMBLE!
ARGH!
MAYBE YOU SHOULDN'T USE THIS PART OF YOUR LAIR, SKUNKY. THE GROUND IS **FAR** TOO UNSTABLE.
HNUHFF!
WHAT DO YOU KEEP IN HERE, ANYWAY?
CHUNK! CHUN CHU
NOT THE SAUSAGES!!
GRAB!
YEEK!
I DIDN'T KNOW ANYTHING WAS DOWN THERE.
OH, AS IF, SKUNKY!
AN ENORMOUS CAVERN UNDER YOUR LAIR, ARE YOU SERIOUSLY TELLING ME YOU'RE NOT HIDING SOME TERRIBLE SECR...
CHUNK! CHUNK! CHUNK!
...WHAT'S THAT SMELL?
CHUNK! CHUNK!
AUGH! WHAT IS THAT? PULL ME UP!!
THEY'RE ONLY SAUSAGES!
CHUNK CHU
THEY'RE NOT STRONG ENOUGH TO SUPPORT A...

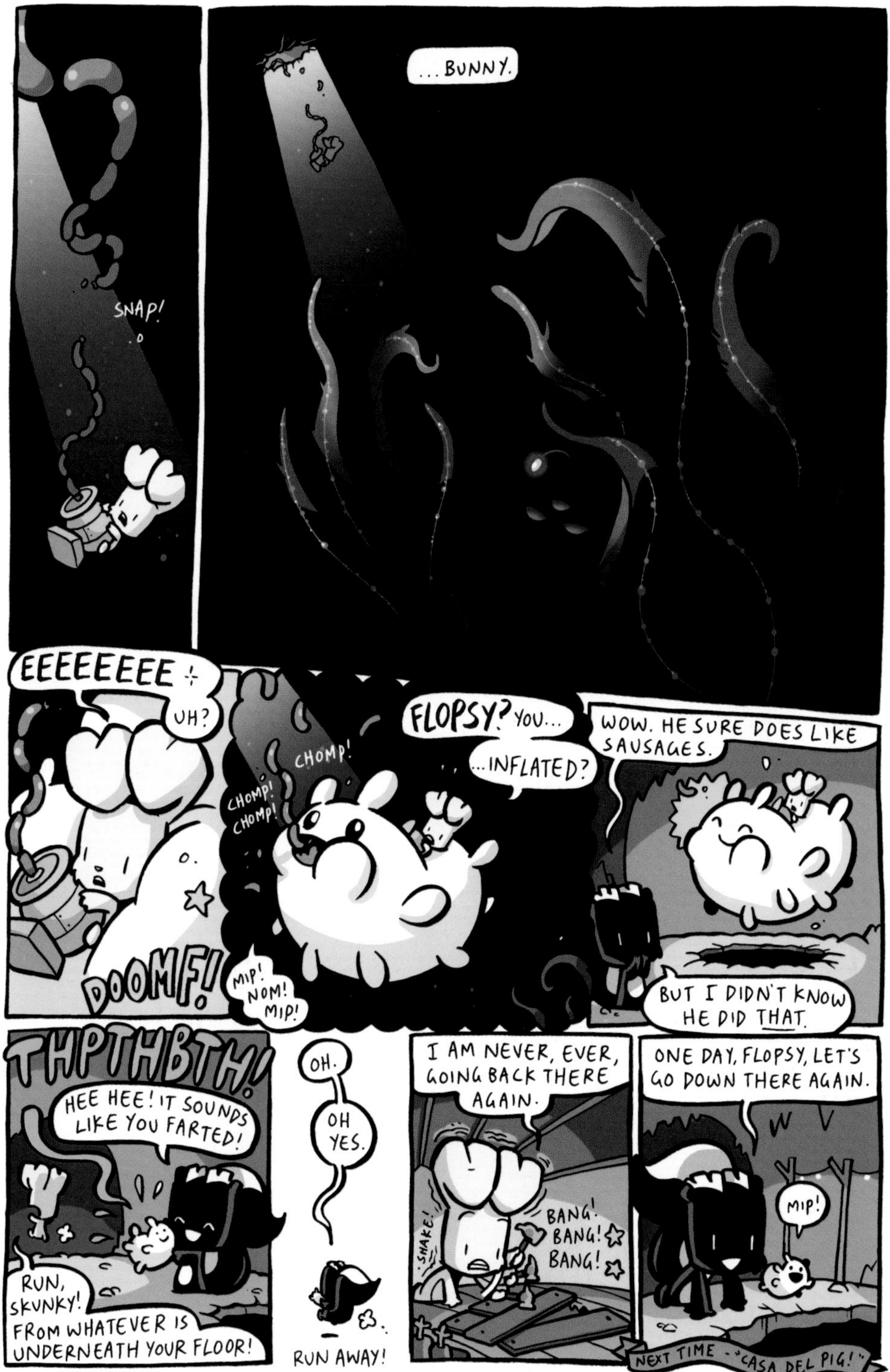
SNAP!
...BUNNY.
EEEEEEEE
UH?
DOOMF!
CHOMP!
CHOMP! CHOMP!
FLOPSY? YOU...
...INFLATED?
MIP! NOM! MIP!
WOW. HE SURE DOES LIKE SAUSAGES.
BUT I DIDN'T KNOW HE DID THAT.
THPTHBTH!
HEE HEE! IT SOUNDS LIKE YOU FARTED!
RUN, SKUNKY!
FROM WHATEVER IS UNDERNEATH YOUR FLOOR!
OH.
OH YES.
RUN AWAY!
I AM NEVER, EVER, GOING BACK THERE AGAIN.
SHAKE!
BANG! BANG! BANG!
ONE DAY, FLOPSY, LET'S GO DOWN THERE AGAIN.
MIP!
NEXT TIME - "CASA DEL PIG!"

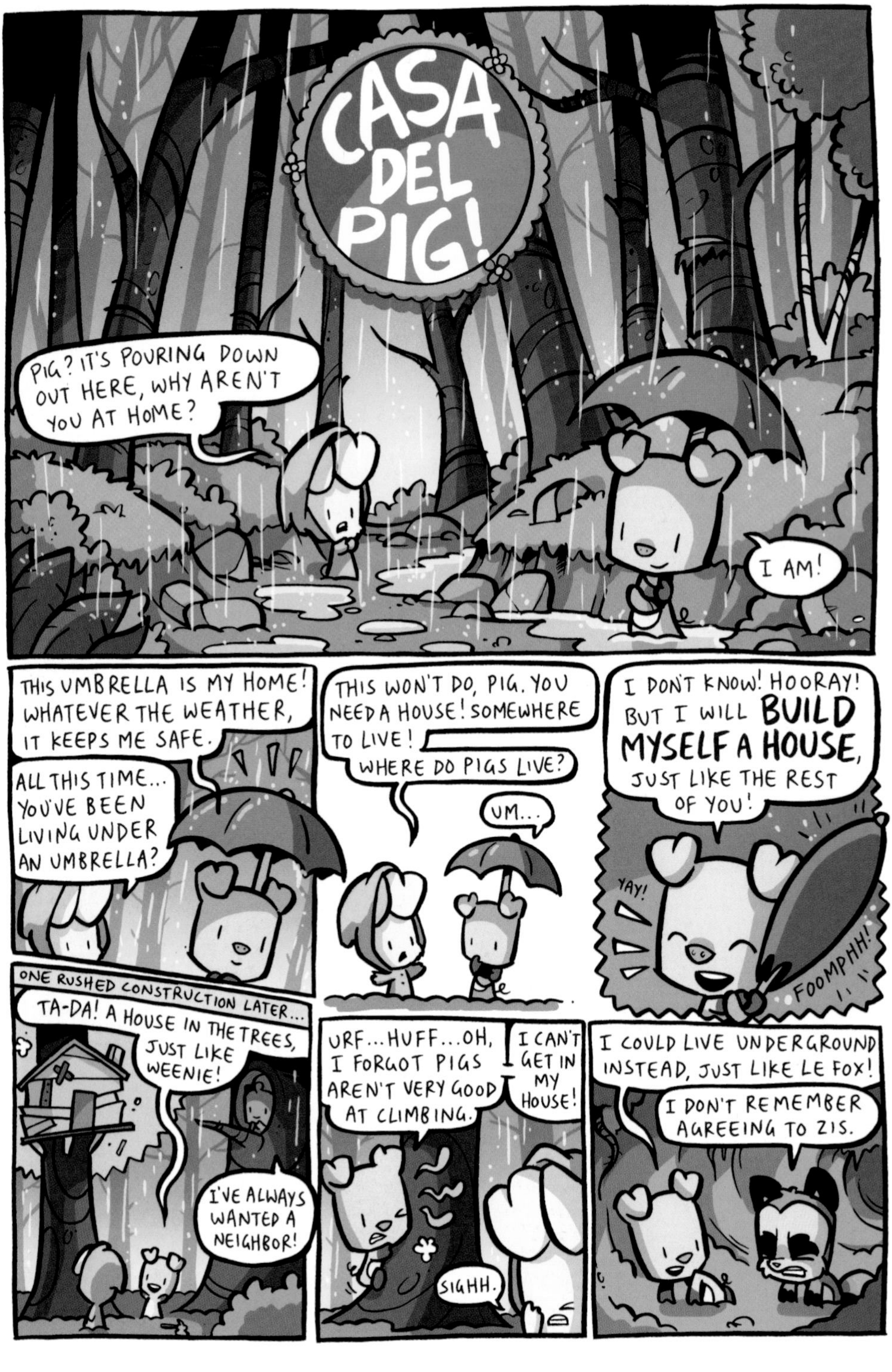
CASA DEL PIG!
PIG? IT'S POURING DOWN OUT HERE, WHY AREN'T YOU AT HOME?
I AM!
THIS UMBRELLA IS MY HOME! WHATEVER THE WEATHER, IT KEEPS ME SAFE.
ALL THIS TIME... YOU'VE BEEN LIVING UNDER AN UMBRELLA?
THIS WON'T DO, PIG. YOU NEED A HOUSE! SOMEWHERE TO LIVE!
WHERE DO PIGS LIVE?
UM...
I DON'T KNOW! HOORAY! BUT I WILL BUILD MYSELF A HOUSE, JUST LIKE THE REST OF YOU!
YAY!
FOOMPHH!
ONE RUSHED CONSTRUCTION LATER...
TA-DA! A HOUSE IN THE TREES, JUST LIKE WEENIE!
I'VE ALWAYS WANTED A NEIGHBOR!
URF...HUFF...OH, I FORGOT PIGS AREN'T VERY GOOD AT CLIMBING.
I CAN'T GET IN MY HOUSE!
SIGHH.
I COULD LIVE UNDERGROUND INSTEAD, JUST LIKE LE FOX!
I DON'T REMEMBER AGREEING TO ZIS.

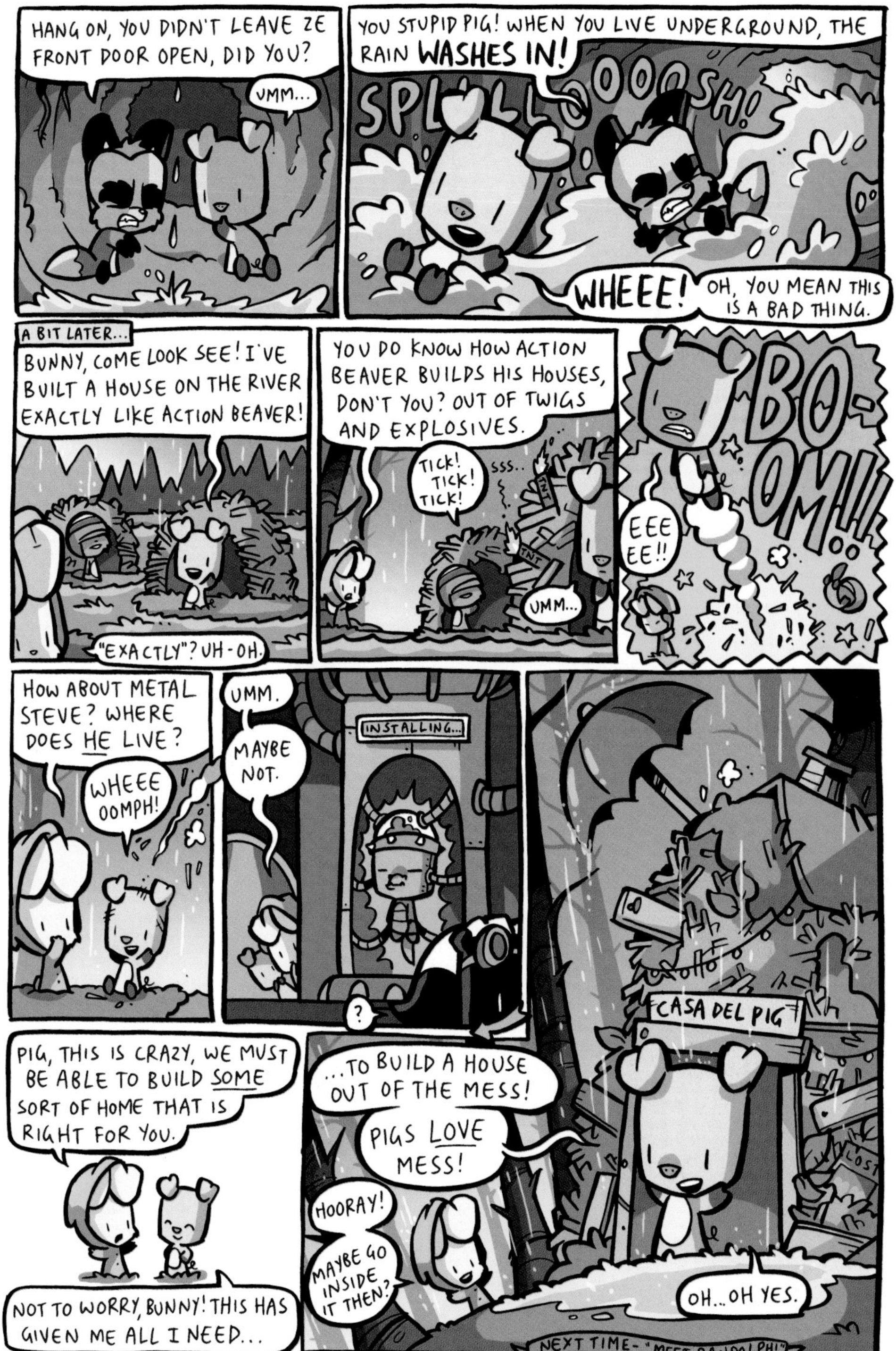
HANG ON, YOU DIDN'T LEAVE ZE FRONT DOOR OPEN, DID YOU?
UMM...
YOU STUPID PIG! WHEN YOU LIVE UNDERGROUND, THE RAIN WASHES IN!
SPLLLOOOOOSH!
WHEEE!
OH, YOU MEAN THIS IS A BAD THING.
A BIT LATER...
BUNNY, COME LOOK SEE! I'VE BUILT A HOUSE ON THE RIVER EXACTLY LIKE ACTION BEAVER!
"EXACTLY"? UH-OH.
YOU DO KNOW HOW ACTION BEAVER BUILDS HIS HOUSES, DON'T YOU? OUT OF TWIGS AND EXPLOSIVES.
TICK! TICK! TICK!
SSS..
TNT
TNT
UMM...
BO-OM!!!
EEE EE!!
HOW ABOUT METAL STEVE? WHERE DOES HE LIVE?
WHEEE OOMPH!
UMM.
MAYBE NOT.
INSTALLING...
?
CASA DEL PIG
PIG, THIS IS CRAZY, WE MUST BE ABLE TO BUILD SOME SORT OF HOME THAT IS RIGHT FOR YOU.
NOT TO WORRY, BUNNY! THIS HAS GIVEN ME ALL I NEED...
...TO BUILD A HOUSE OUT OF THE MESS!
PIGS LOVE MESS!
HOORAY!
MAYBE GO INSIDE IT THEN?
OH...OH YES.
NEXT TIME - "MEET RANDOLPH!"

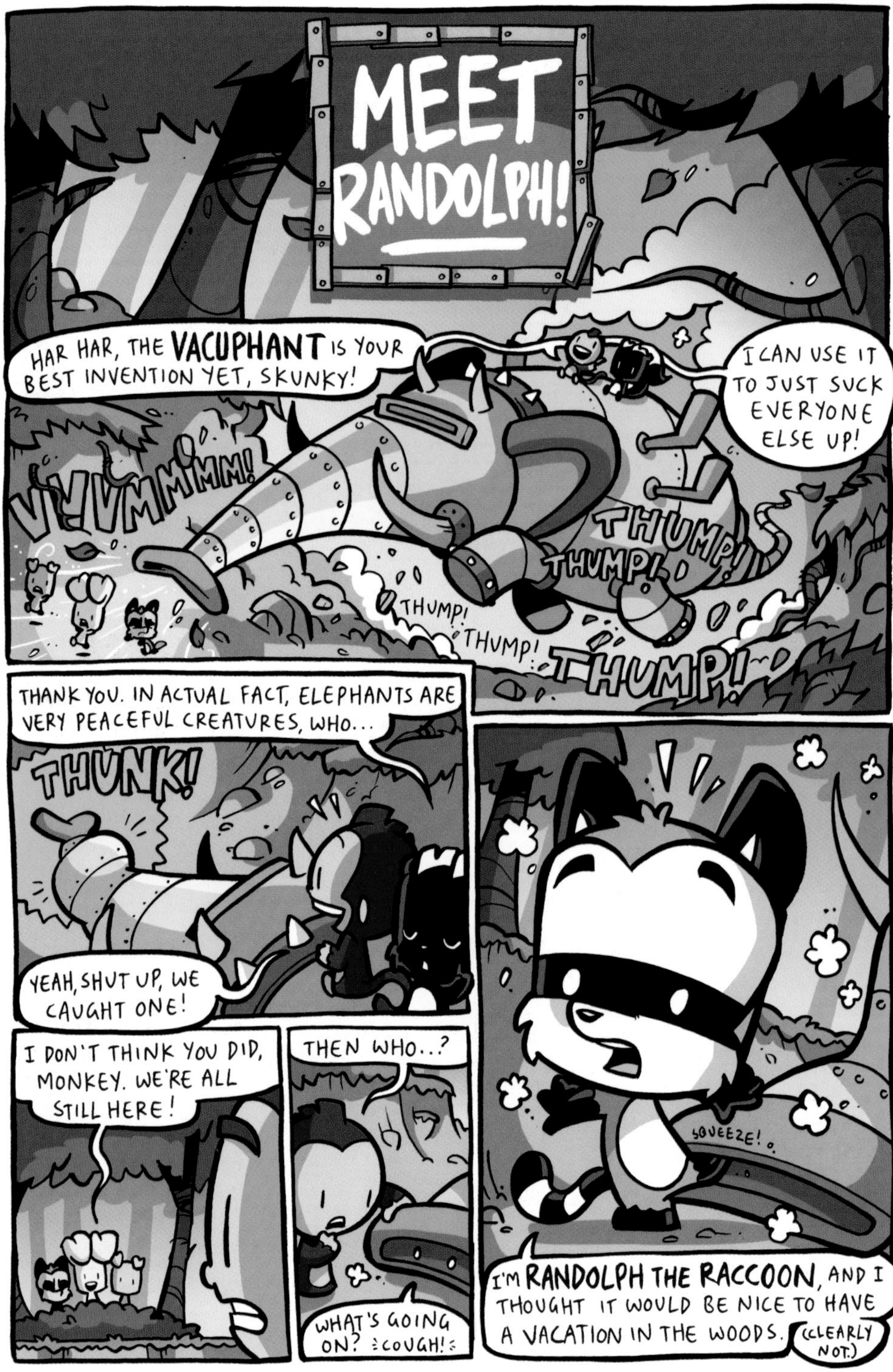
MEET RANDOLPH!
HAR HAR, THE VACUPHANT IS YOUR BEST INVENTION YET, SKUNKY!
I CAN USE IT TO JUST SUCK EVERYONE ELSE UP!
VVVMMMMM!
THUMP! THUMP!
THUMP! THUMP! THUMP!
THANK YOU. IN ACTUAL FACT, ELEPHANTS ARE VERY PEACEFUL CREATURES, WHO...
THUNK!
YEAH, SHUT UP, WE CAUGHT ONE!
I DON'T THINK YOU DID, MONKEY. WE'RE ALL STILL HERE!
THEN WHO...?
WHAT'S GOING ON? COUGH!
SQUEEZE!
I'M RANDOLPH THE RACCOON, AND I THOUGHT IT WOULD BE NICE TO HAVE A VACATION IN THE WOODS.
(CLEARLY NOT.)

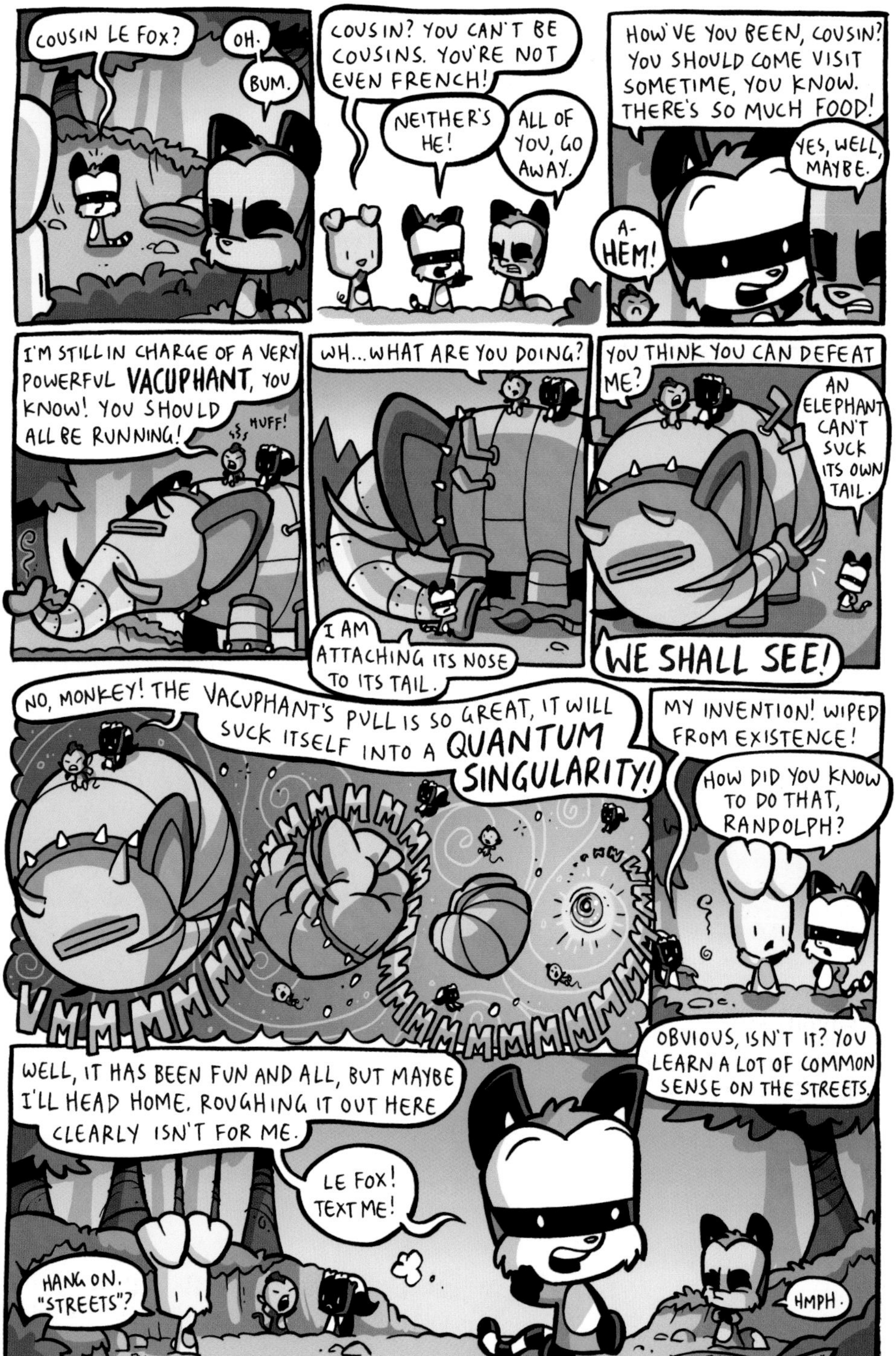
COUSIN LE FOX?
OH.
BUM.
COUSIN? YOU CAN'T BE COUSINS. YOU'RE NOT EVEN FRENCH!
NEITHER'S HE!
ALL OF YOU, GO AWAY.
HOW'VE YOU BEEN, COUSIN? YOU SHOULD COME VISIT SOMETIME, YOU KNOW. THERE'S SO MUCH FOOD!
YES, WELL, MAYBE.
A-HEM!
I'M STILL IN CHARGE OF A VERY POWERFUL VACUPHANT, YOU KNOW! YOU SHOULD ALL BE RUNNING!
HUFF!
WH... WHAT ARE YOU DOING?
I AM ATTACHING ITS NOSE TO ITS TAIL.
YOU THINK YOU CAN DEFEAT ME?
AN ELEPHANT CAN'T SUCK ITS OWN TAIL.
WE SHALL SEE!
NO, MONKEY! THE VACUPHANT'S PULL IS SO GREAT, IT WILL SUCK ITSELF INTO A QUANTUM SINGULARITY!
VMMMMMMMMMMMMMMMMMMMMMMMMMMMMMMMMM
MY INVENTION! WIPED FROM EXISTENCE!
HOW DID YOU KNOW TO DO THAT, RANDOLPH?
OBVIOUS, ISN'T IT? YOU LEARN A LOT OF COMMON SENSE ON THE STREETS.
WELL, IT HAS BEEN FUN AND ALL, BUT MAYBE I'LL HEAD HOME. ROUGHING IT OUT HERE CLEARLY ISN'T FOR ME.
LE FOX! TEXT ME!
HANG ON. "STREETS"?
HMPH.
NEXT TIME - "THE STENCH!"

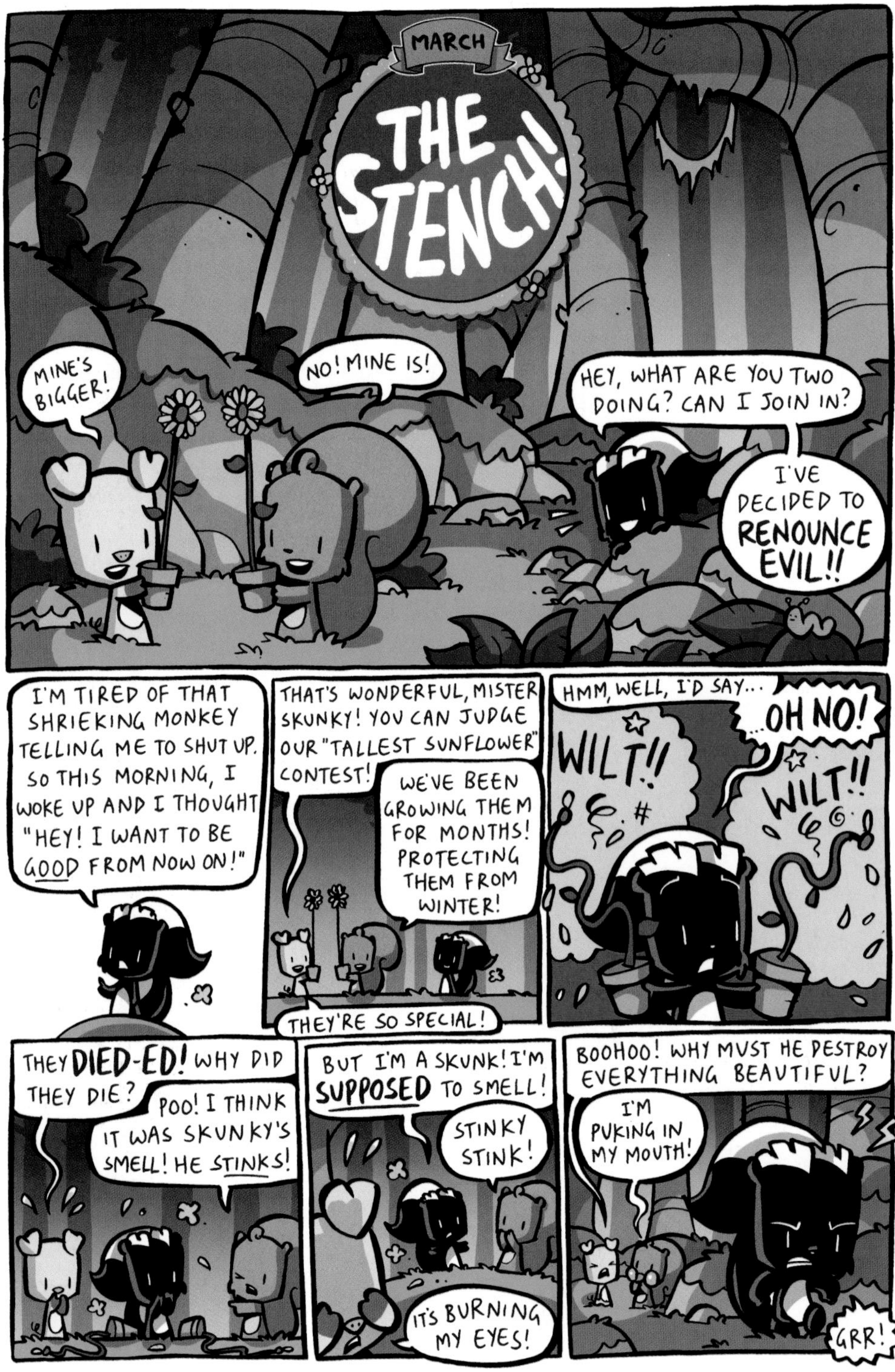
MARCH
THE STENCH!
MINE'S BIGGER!
NO! MINE IS!
HEY, WHAT ARE YOU TWO DOING? CAN I JOIN IN?
I'VE DECIDED TO RENOUNCE EVIL!!
I'M TIRED OF THAT SHRIEKING MONKEY TELLING ME TO SHUT UP. SO THIS MORNING, I WOKE UP AND I THOUGHT "HEY! I WANT TO BE GOOD FROM NOW ON!"
THAT'S WONDERFUL, MISTER SKUNKY! YOU CAN JUDGE OUR "TALLEST SUNFLOWER" CONTEST!
WE'VE BEEN GROWING THEM FOR MONTHS! PROTECTING THEM FROM WINTER!
THEY'RE SO SPECIAL!
HMM, WELL, I'D SAY...
...OH NO!
WILT!!
WILT!!
THEY DIED-ED! WHY DID THEY DIE?
POO! I THINK IT WAS SKUNKY'S SMELL! HE STINKS!
BUT I'M A SKUNK! I'M SUPPOSED TO SMELL!
STINKY STINK!
IT'S BURNING MY EYES!
BOOHOO! WHY MUST HE DESTROY EVERYTHING BEAUTIFUL?
I'M PUKING IN MY MOUTH!
GRR!

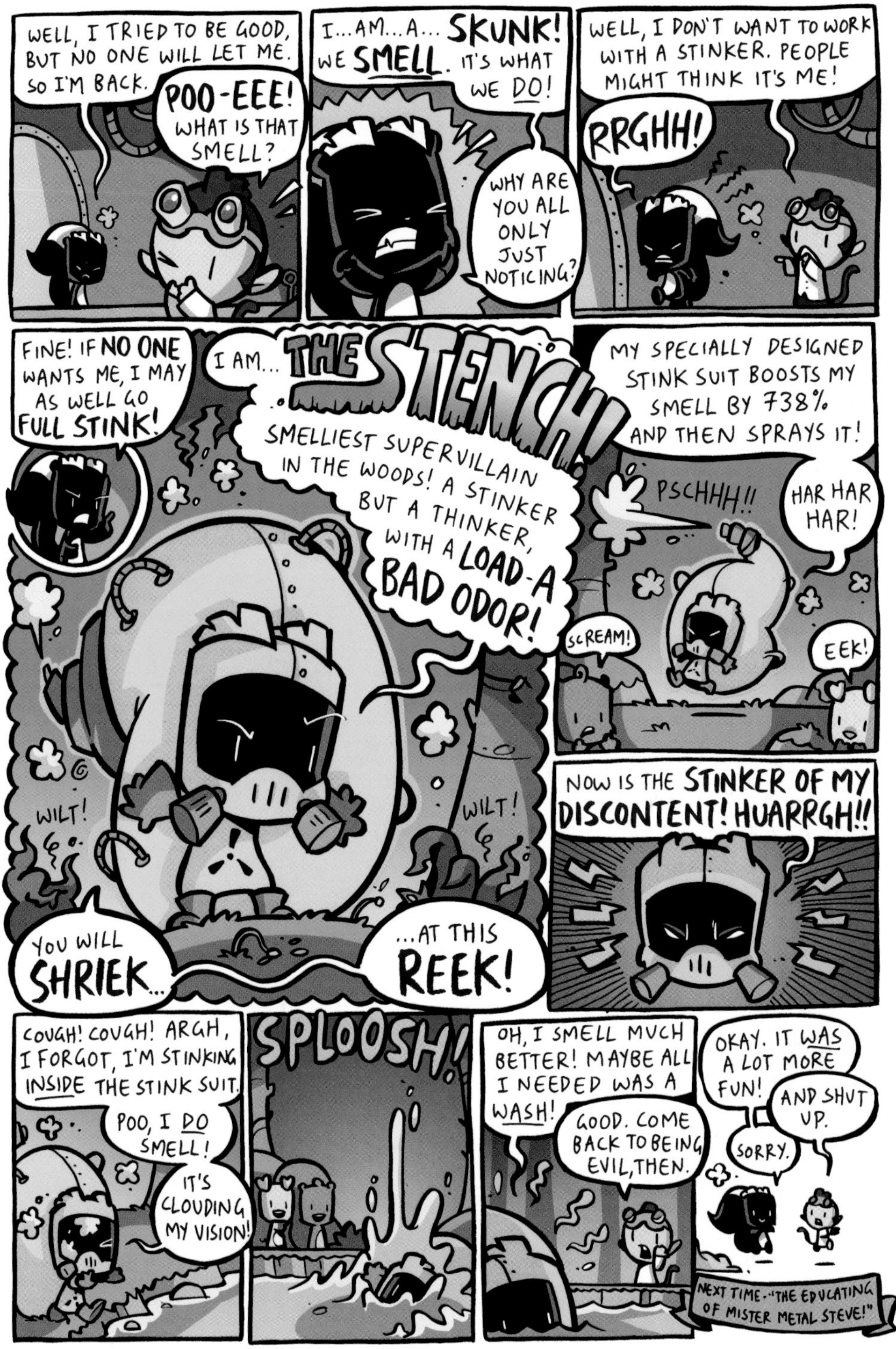
WELL, I TRIED TO BE GOOD, BUT NO ONE WILL LET ME. SO I'M BACK.
POO-EEE! WHAT IS THAT SMELL?
I...AM...A... SKUNK! WE SMELL. IT'S WHAT WE DO!
WHY ARE YOU ALL ONLY JUST NOTICING?
WELL, I DON'T WANT TO WORK WITH A STINKER. PEOPLE MIGHT THINK IT'S ME!
RRGHH!
FINE! IF NO ONE WANTS ME, I MAY AS WELL GO FULL STINK!
I AM... THE STENCH!
SMELLIEST SUPERVILLAIN IN THE WOODS! A STINKER BUT A THINKER, WITH A LOAD-A BAD ODOR!
WILT!
WILT!
YOU WILL SHRIEK...
...AT THIS REEK!
MY SPECIALLY DESIGNED STINK SUIT BOOSTS MY SMELL BY 738% AND THEN SPRAYS IT!
PSCHHH!!
HAR HAR HAR!
SCREAM!
EEK!
NOW IS THE STINKER OF MY DISCONTENT! HUARRGH!!
COUGH! COUGH! ARGH, I FORGOT, I'M STINKING INSIDE THE STINK SUIT.
POO, I DO SMELL!
IT'S CLOUDING MY VISION!
SPLOOSH!
OH, I SMELL MUCH BETTER! MAYBE ALL I NEEDED WAS A WASH!
GOOD. COME BACK TO BEING EVIL, THEN.
OKAY. IT WAS A LOT MORE FUN!
SORRY.
AND SHUT UP.
NEXT TIME - "THE EDUCATING OF MISTER METAL STEVE!"

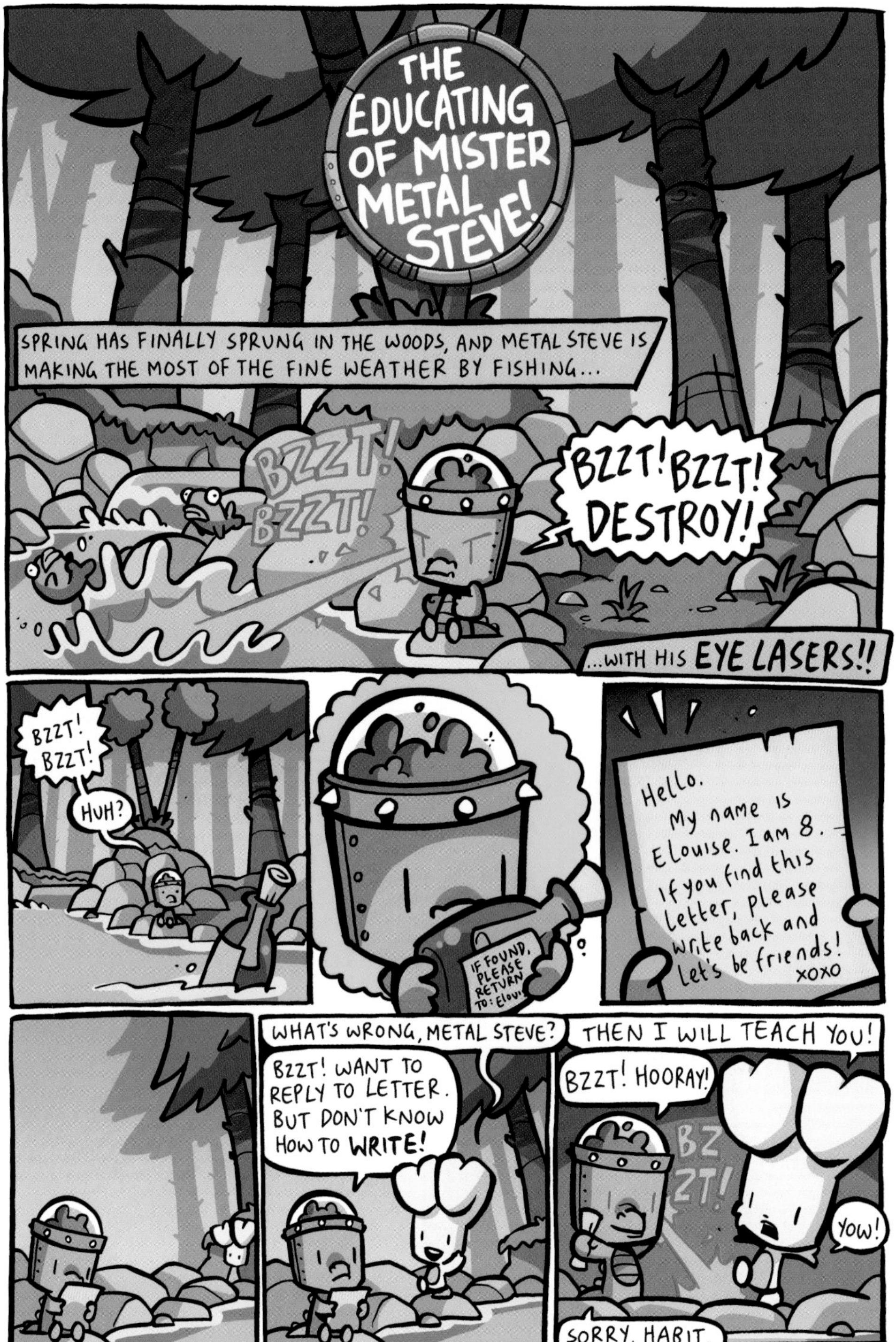
THE EDUCATING OF MISTER METAL STEVE!
SPRING HAS FINALLY SPRUNG IN THE WOODS, AND METAL STEVE IS MAKING THE MOST OF THE FINE WEATHER BY FISHING...
BZZT! BZZT!
BZZT! BZZT! DESTROY!
...WITH HIS EYE LASERS!!
BZZT! BZZT!
HUH?
IF FOUND, PLEASE RETURN TO: ELOUI
Hello. My name is Elouise. I am 8. If you find this letter, please write back and let's be friends! xoxo
WHAT'S WRONG, METAL STEVE?
BZZT! WANT TO REPLY TO LETTER. BUT DON'T KNOW HOW TO WRITE!
THEN I WILL TEACH YOU!
BZZT! HOORAY!
BZZT!
YOW!
SORRY, HABIT.

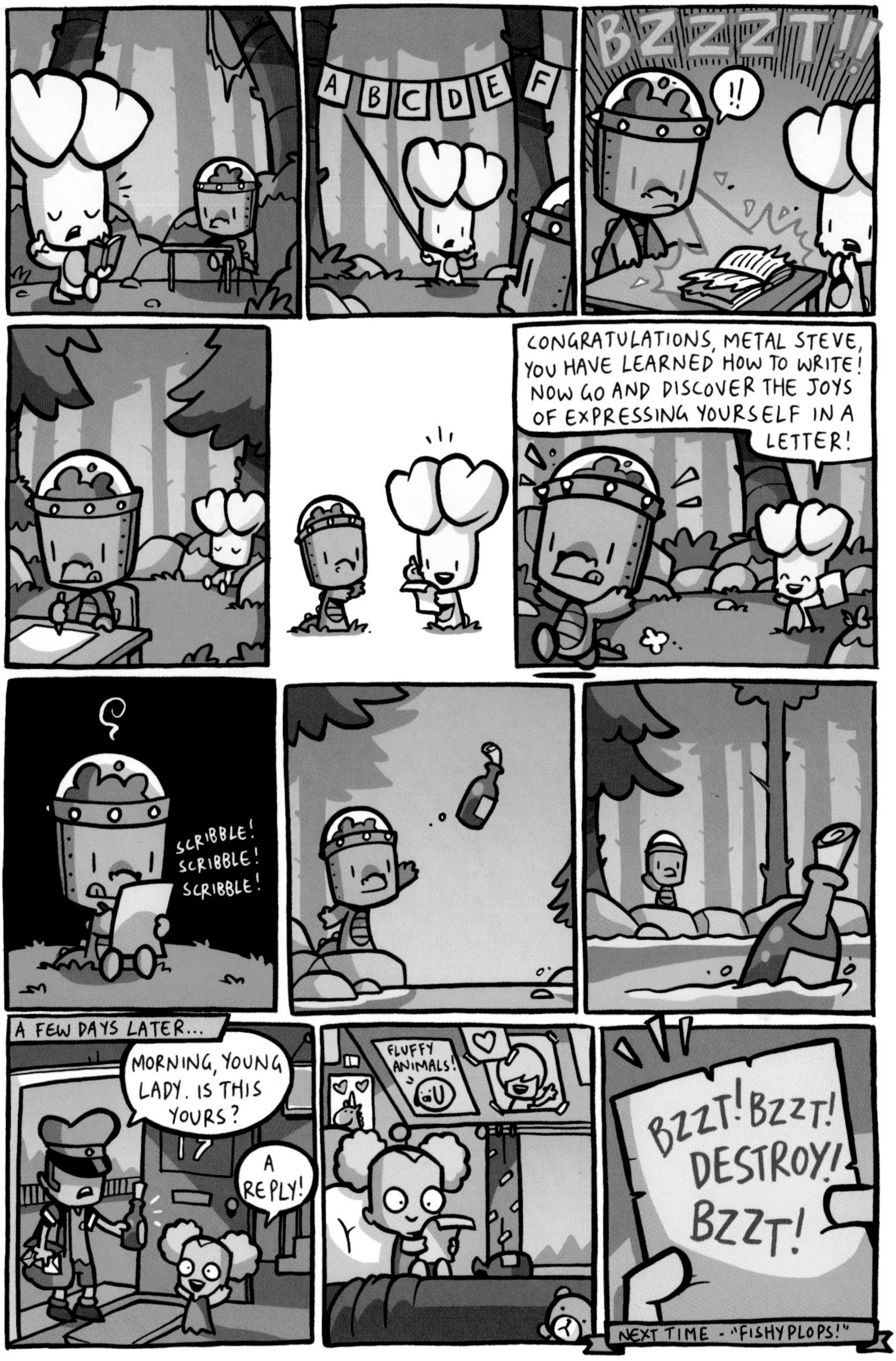
A B C D E F
BZZZT!!
!!
CONGRATULATIONS, METAL STEVE, YOU HAVE LEARNED HOW TO WRITE! NOW GO AND DISCOVER THE JOYS OF EXPRESSING YOURSELF IN A LETTER!
SCRIBBLE! SCRIBBLE! SCRIBBLE!
A FEW DAYS LATER...
MORNING, YOUNG LADY. IS THIS YOURS?
17
A REPLY!
FLUFFY ANIMALS!
BZZT! BZZT! DESTROY! BZZT!
NEXT TIME - "FISHYPLOPS!"

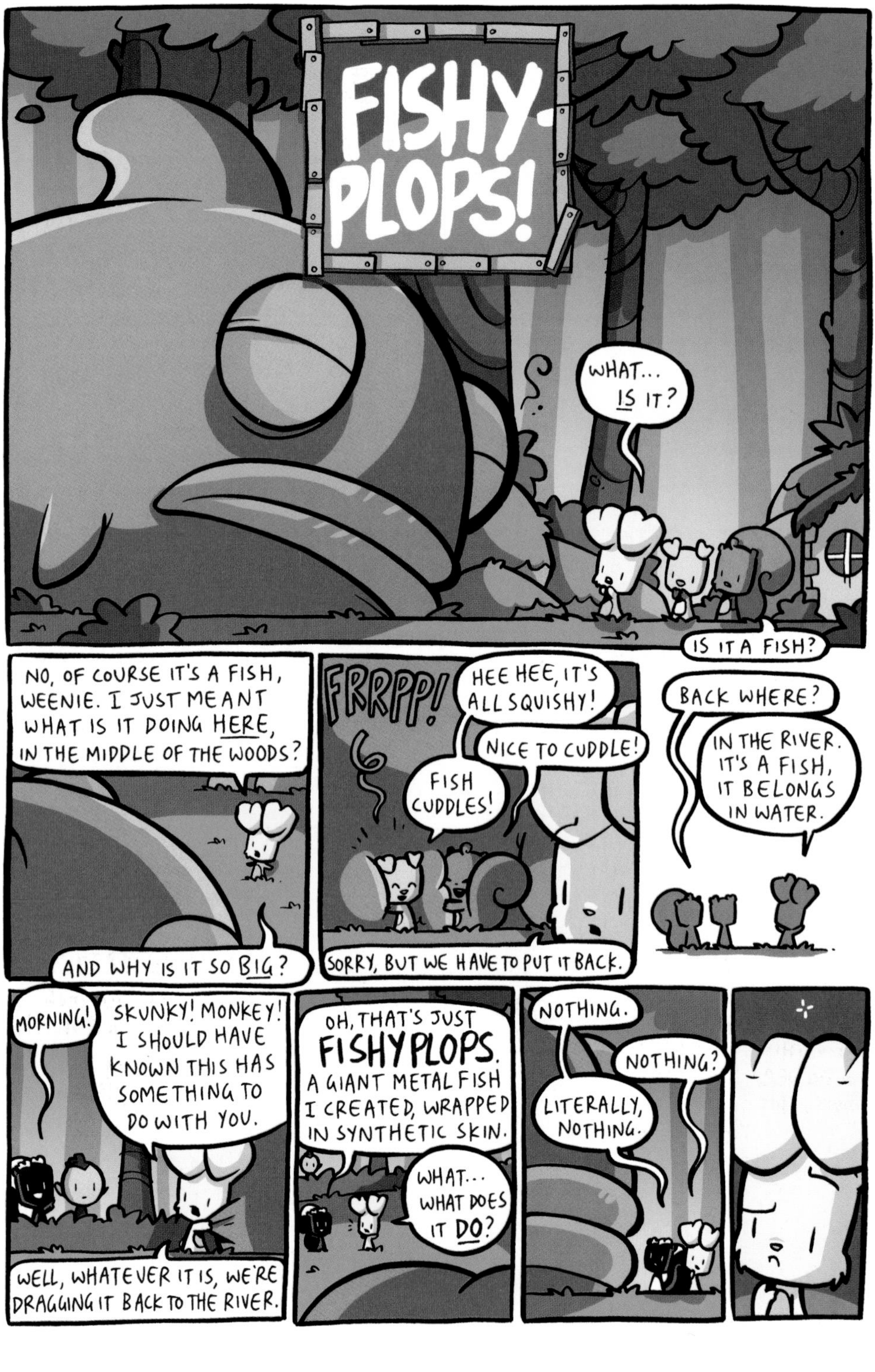
FISHY-PLOPS!
WHAT... IS IT?
IS IT A FISH?
NO, OF COURSE IT'S A FISH, WEENIE. I JUST MEANT WHAT IS IT DOING HERE, IN THE MIDDLE OF THE WOODS?
AND WHY IS IT SO BIG?
FRRPP!
HEE HEE, IT'S ALL SQUISHY!
NICE TO CUDDLE!
FISH CUDDLES!
SORRY, BUT WE HAVE TO PUT IT BACK.
BACK WHERE?
IN THE RIVER. IT'S A FISH, IT BELONGS IN WATER.
MORNING!
SKUNKY! MONKEY! I SHOULD HAVE KNOWN THIS HAS SOMETHING TO DO WITH YOU.
WELL, WHATEVER IT IS, WE'RE DRAGGING IT BACK TO THE RIVER.
OH, THAT'S JUST FISHYPLOPS. A GIANT METAL FISH I CREATED, WRAPPED IN SYNTHETIC SKIN.
WHAT... WHAT DOES IT DO?
NOTHING.
NOTHING?
LITERALLY, NOTHING.

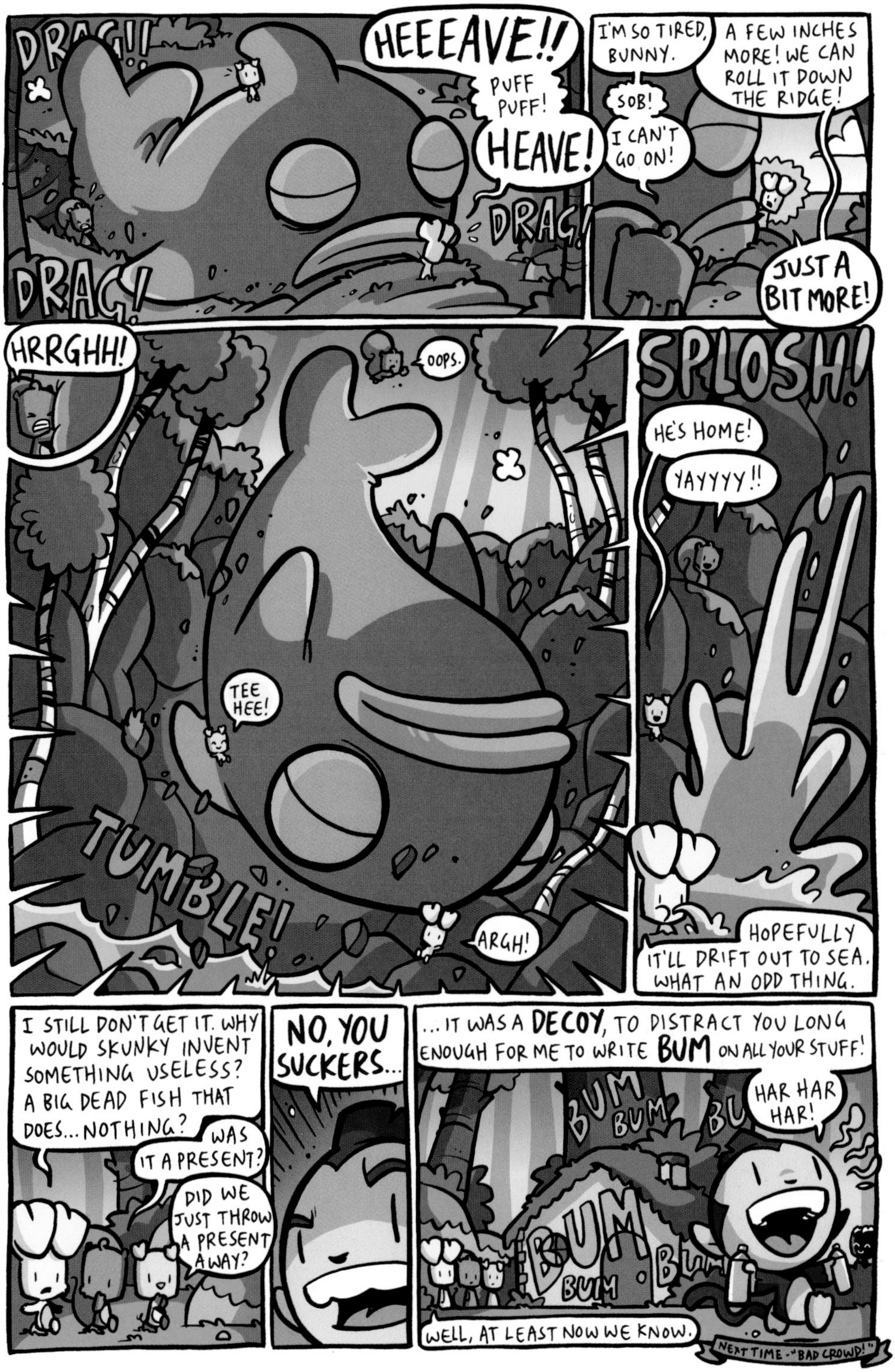
DRAG!!
HEEEAVE!!
PUFF PUFF!
HEAVE!
DRAG!
DRAG!
I'M SO TIRED, BUNNY.
SOB!
I CAN'T GO ON!
A FEW INCHES MORE! WE CAN ROLL IT DOWN THE RIDGE!
JUST A BIT MORE!
HRRGHH!
OOPS.
TEE HEE!
TUMBLE!
ARGH!
SPLOSH!
HE'S HOME!
YAYYYY!!
HOPEFULLY IT'LL DRIFT OUT TO SEA. WHAT AN ODD THING.
I STILL DON'T GET IT. WHY WOULD SKUNKY INVENT SOMETHING USELESS? A BIG DEAD FISH THAT DOES... NOTHING?
WAS IT A PRESENT?
DID WE JUST THROW A PRESENT AWAY?
NO, YOU SUCKERS...
...IT WAS A DECOY, TO DISTRACT YOU LONG ENOUGH FOR ME TO WRITE BUM ON ALL YOUR STUFF!
BUM
BUM
HAR HAR HAR!
BUM
BUM
WELL, AT LEAST NOW WE KNOW.
NEXT TIME - "BAD CROWD!"

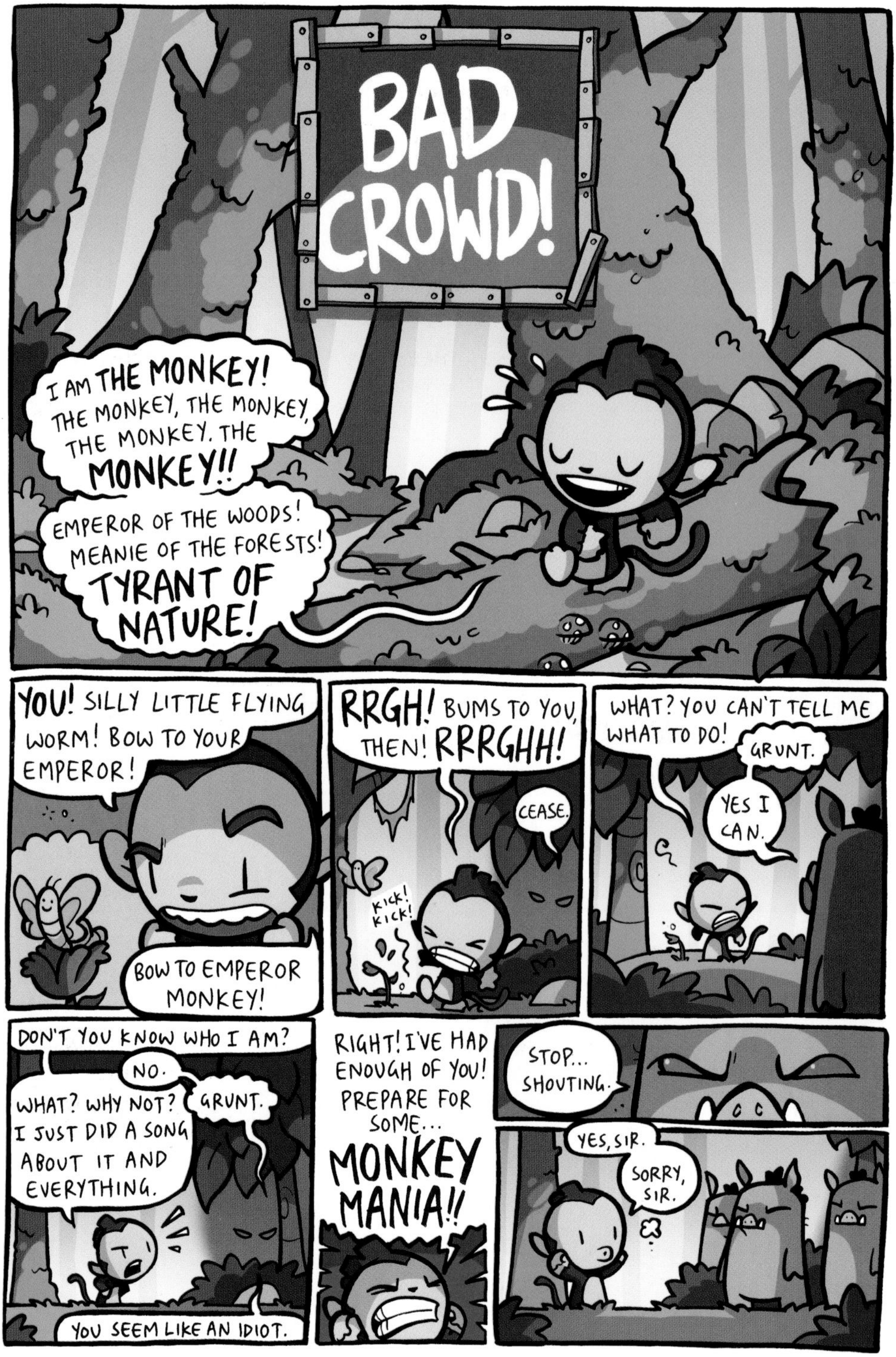

BAD CROWD!
I AM THE MONKEY! THE MONKEY, THE MONKEY, THE MONKEY. THE MONKEY!!
EMPEROR OF THE WOODS! MEANIE OF THE FORESTS! TYRANT OF NATURE!
YOU! SILLY LITTLE FLYING WORM! BOW TO YOUR EMPEROR!
BOW TO EMPEROR MONKEY!
RRGH! BUMS TO YOU, THEN! RRRGHH!
CEASE.
KICK! KICK!
WHAT? YOU CAN'T TELL ME WHAT TO DO!
GRUNT.
YES I CAN.
DON'T YOU KNOW WHO I AM?
NO.
WHAT? WHY NOT? I JUST DID A SONG ABOUT IT AND EVERYTHING.
GRUNT.
YOU SEEM LIKE AN IDIOT.
RIGHT! I'VE HAD ENOUGH OF YOU! PREPARE FOR SOME...
MONKEY MANIA!!
STOP... SHOUTING.
YES, SIR.
SORRY, SIR.

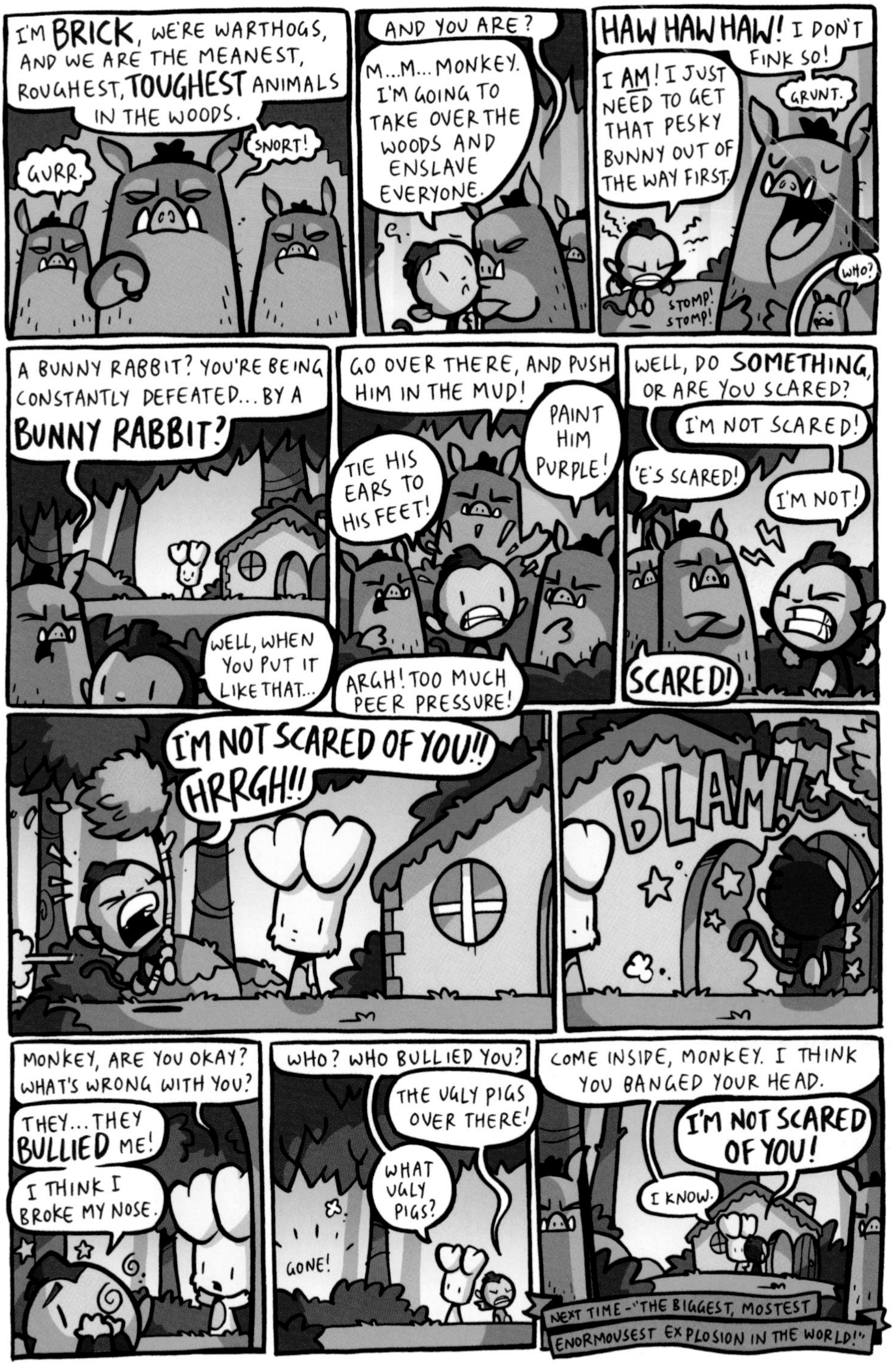

I'M BRICK, WE'RE WARTHOGS, AND WE ARE THE MEANEST, ROUGHEST, TOUGHEST ANIMALS IN THE WOODS.
GURR.
SNORT!
AND YOU ARE?
M...M...MONKEY. I'M GOING TO TAKE OVER THE WOODS AND ENSLAVE EVERYONE.
HAW HAW HAW! I DON'T FINK SO!
GRUNT.
I AM! I JUST NEED TO GET THAT PESKY BUNNY OUT OF THE WAY FIRST.
STOMP! STOMP!
WHO?
A BUNNY RABBIT? YOU'RE BEING CONSTANTLY DEFEATED... BY A BUNNY RABBIT?
WELL, WHEN YOU PUT IT LIKE THAT...
GO OVER THERE, AND PUSH HIM IN THE MUD!
PAINT HIM PURPLE!
TIE HIS EARS TO HIS FEET!
ARGH! TOO MUCH PEER PRESSURE!
WELL, DO SOMETHING, OR ARE YOU SCARED?
I'M NOT SCARED!
'E'S SCARED!
I'M NOT!
SCARED!
I'M NOT SCARED OF YOU!! HRRGH!!
BLAM!
MONKEY, ARE YOU OKAY? WHAT'S WRONG WITH YOU?
THEY...THEY BULLIED ME!
I THINK I BROKE MY NOSE.
WHO? WHO BULLIED YOU?
THE UGLY PIGS OVER THERE!
WHAT UGLY PIGS?
GONE!
COME INSIDE, MONKEY. I THINK YOU BANGED YOUR HEAD.
I'M NOT SCARED OF YOU!
I KNOW.
NEXT TIME–"THE BIGGEST, MOSTEST ENORMOUSEST EXPLOSION IN THE WORLD!"

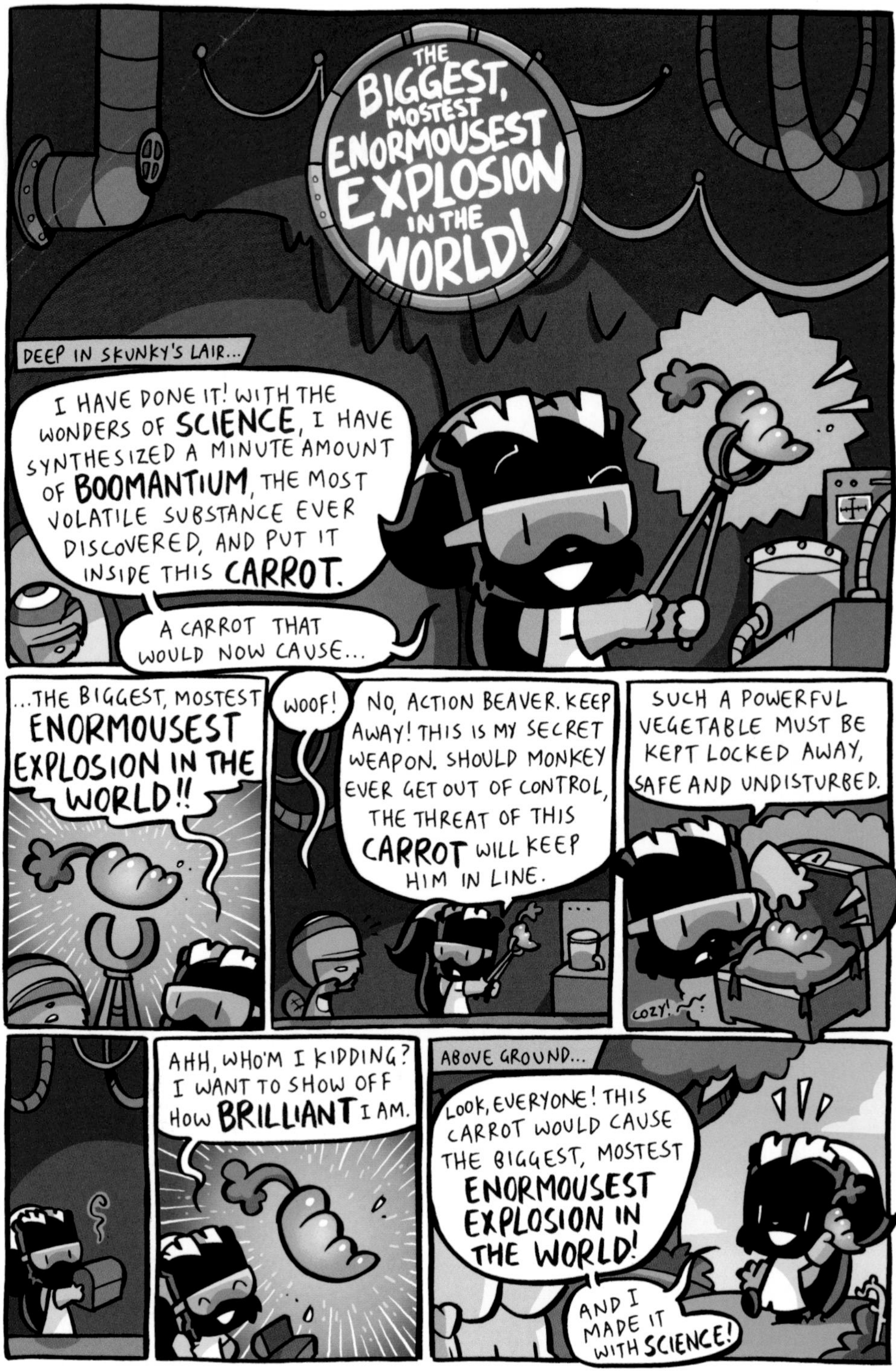
THE BIGGEST, MOSTEST ENORMOUSEST EXPLOSION IN THE WORLD!
DEEP IN SKUNKY'S LAIR...
I HAVE DONE IT! WITH THE WONDERS OF SCIENCE, I HAVE SYNTHESIZED A MINUTE AMOUNT OF BOOMANTIUM, THE MOST VOLATILE SUBSTANCE EVER DISCOVERED, AND PUT IT INSIDE THIS CARROT.
A CARROT THAT WOULD NOW CAUSE...
...THE BIGGEST, MOSTEST ENORMOUSEST EXPLOSION IN THE WORLD!!
WOOF!
NO, ACTION BEAVER. KEEP AWAY! THIS IS MY SECRET WEAPON. SHOULD MONKEY EVER GET OUT OF CONTROL, THE THREAT OF THIS CARROT WILL KEEP HIM IN LINE.
SUCH A POWERFUL VEGETABLE MUST BE KEPT LOCKED AWAY, SAFE AND UNDISTURBED.
COZY!
AHH, WHO'M I KIDDING? I WANT TO SHOW OFF HOW BRILLIANT I AM.
ABOVE GROUND...
LOOK, EVERYONE! THIS CARROT WOULD CAUSE THE BIGGEST, MOSTEST ENORMOUSEST EXPLOSION IN THE WORLD!
AND I MADE IT WITH SCIENCE!

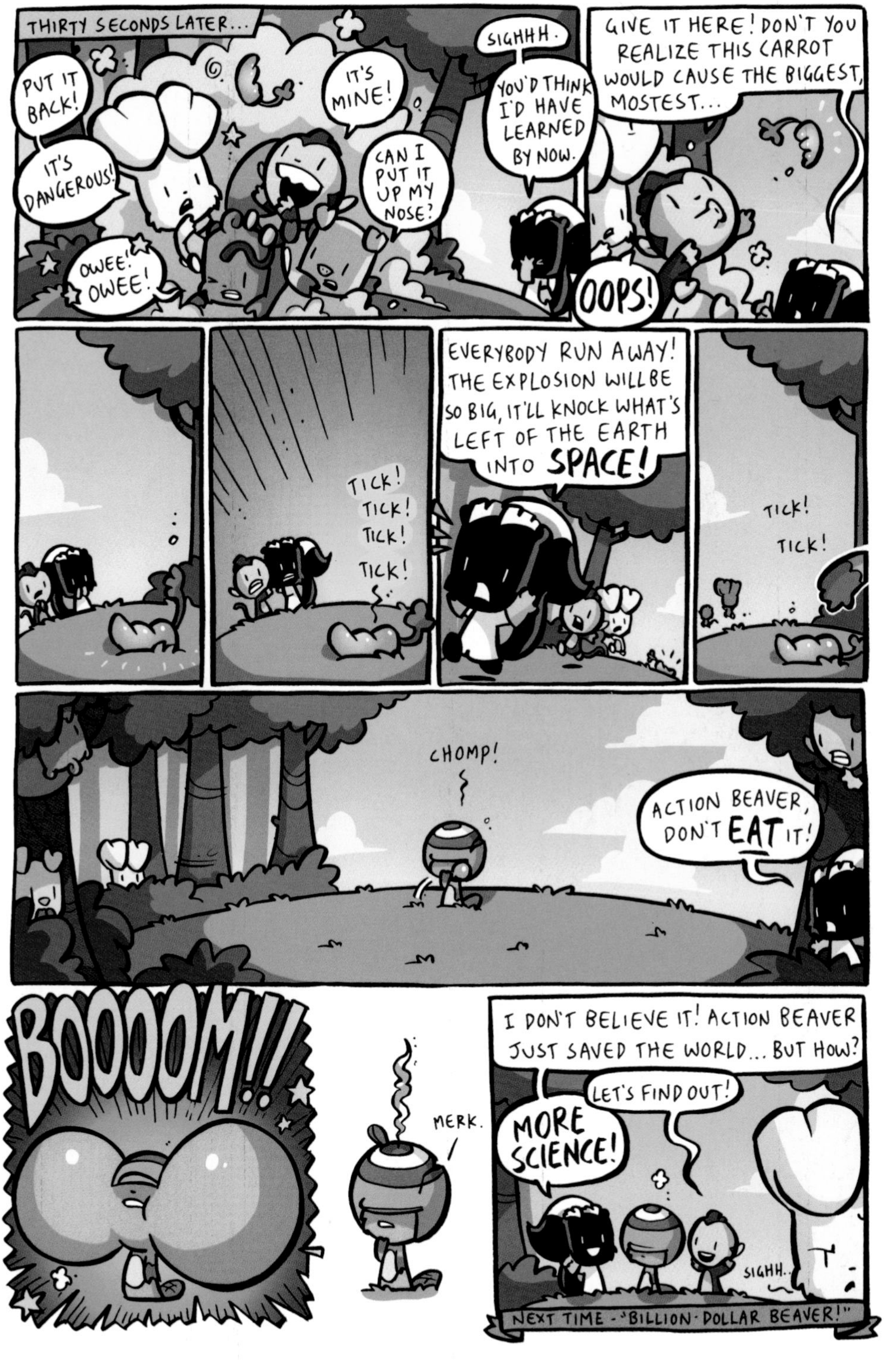
THIRTY SECONDS LATER...
PUT IT BACK!
IT'S DANGEROUS!
IT'S MINE!
OWEE! OWEE!
CAN I PUT IT UP MY NOSE?
SIGHHH.
YOU'D THINK I'D HAVE LEARNED BY NOW.
GIVE IT HERE! DON'T YOU REALIZE THIS CARROT WOULD CAUSE THE BIGGEST, MOSTEST...
OOPS!
TICK! TICK! TICK! TICK!
EVERYBODY RUN AWAY! THE EXPLOSION WILL BE SO BIG, IT'LL KNOCK WHAT'S LEFT OF THE EARTH INTO SPACE!
TICK! TICK!
CHOMP!
ACTION BEAVER, DON'T EAT IT!
BOOOOM!!
MERK.
I DON'T BELIEVE IT! ACTION BEAVER JUST SAVED THE WORLD... BUT HOW?
LET'S FIND OUT!
MORE SCIENCE!
SIGHH.
NEXT TIME - "BILLION-DOLLAR BEAVER!"

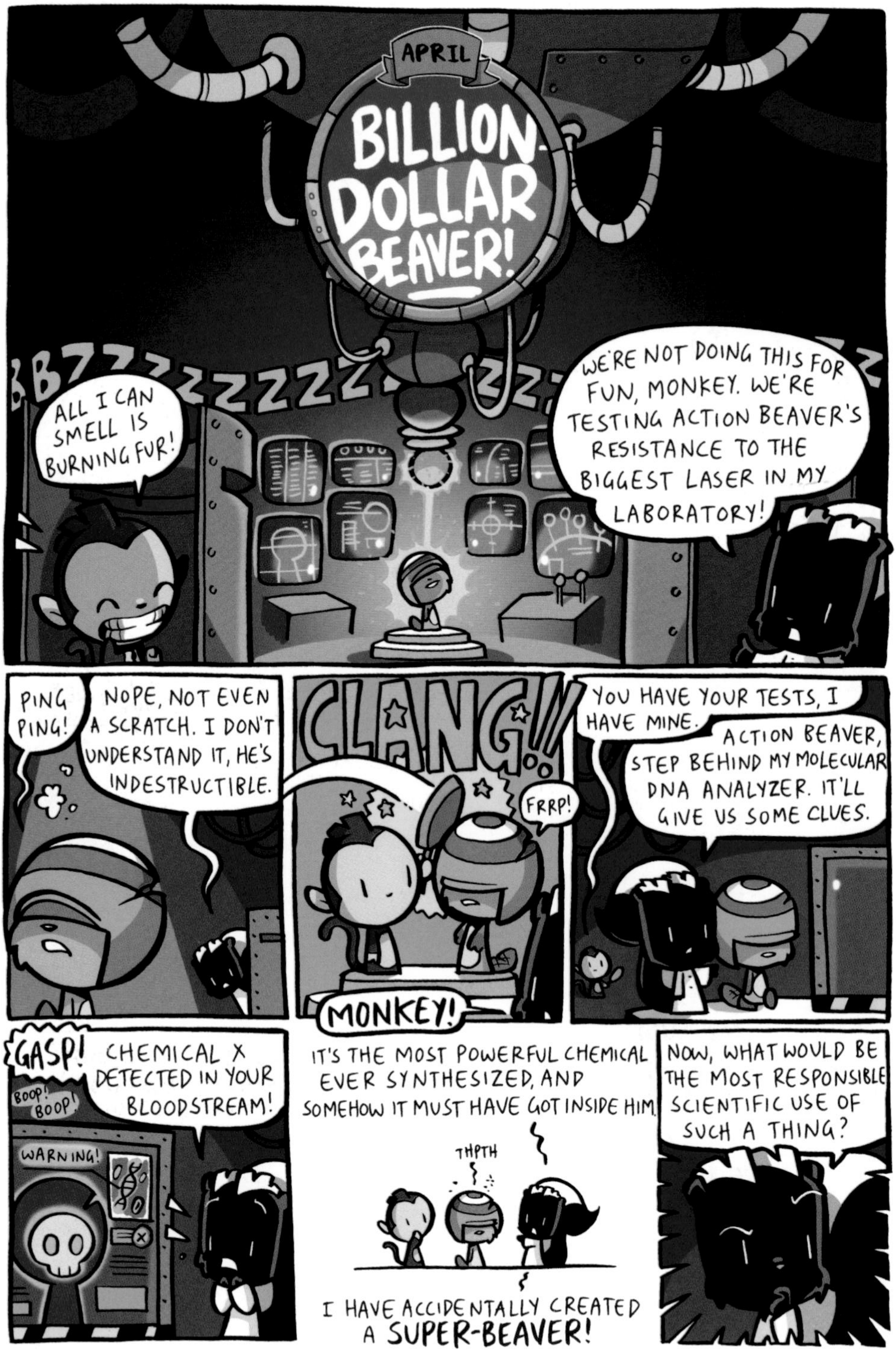
APRIL
BILLION-DOLLAR BEAVER!
BZZZZZZZZZZZZZZ
ALL I CAN SMELL IS BURNING FUR!
WE'RE NOT DOING THIS FOR FUN, MONKEY. WE'RE TESTING ACTION BEAVER'S RESISTANCE TO THE BIGGEST LASER IN MY LABORATORY!
PING PING!
NOPE, NOT EVEN A SCRATCH. I DON'T UNDERSTAND IT, HE'S INDESTRUCTIBLE.
CLANG!!
FRRP!
MONKEY!
YOU HAVE YOUR TESTS, I HAVE MINE.
ACTION BEAVER, STEP BEHIND MY MOLECULAR DNA ANALYZER. IT'LL GIVE US SOME CLUES.
GASP!
CHEMICAL X DETECTED IN YOUR BLOODSTREAM!
BOOP! BOOP!
WARNING!
IT'S THE MOST POWERFUL CHEMICAL EVER SYNTHESIZED, AND SOMEHOW IT MUST HAVE GOT INSIDE HIM.
THPTH
I HAVE ACCIDENTALLY CREATED A SUPER-BEAVER!
NOW, WHAT WOULD BE THE MOST RESPONSIBLE SCIENTIFIC USE OF SUCH A THING?

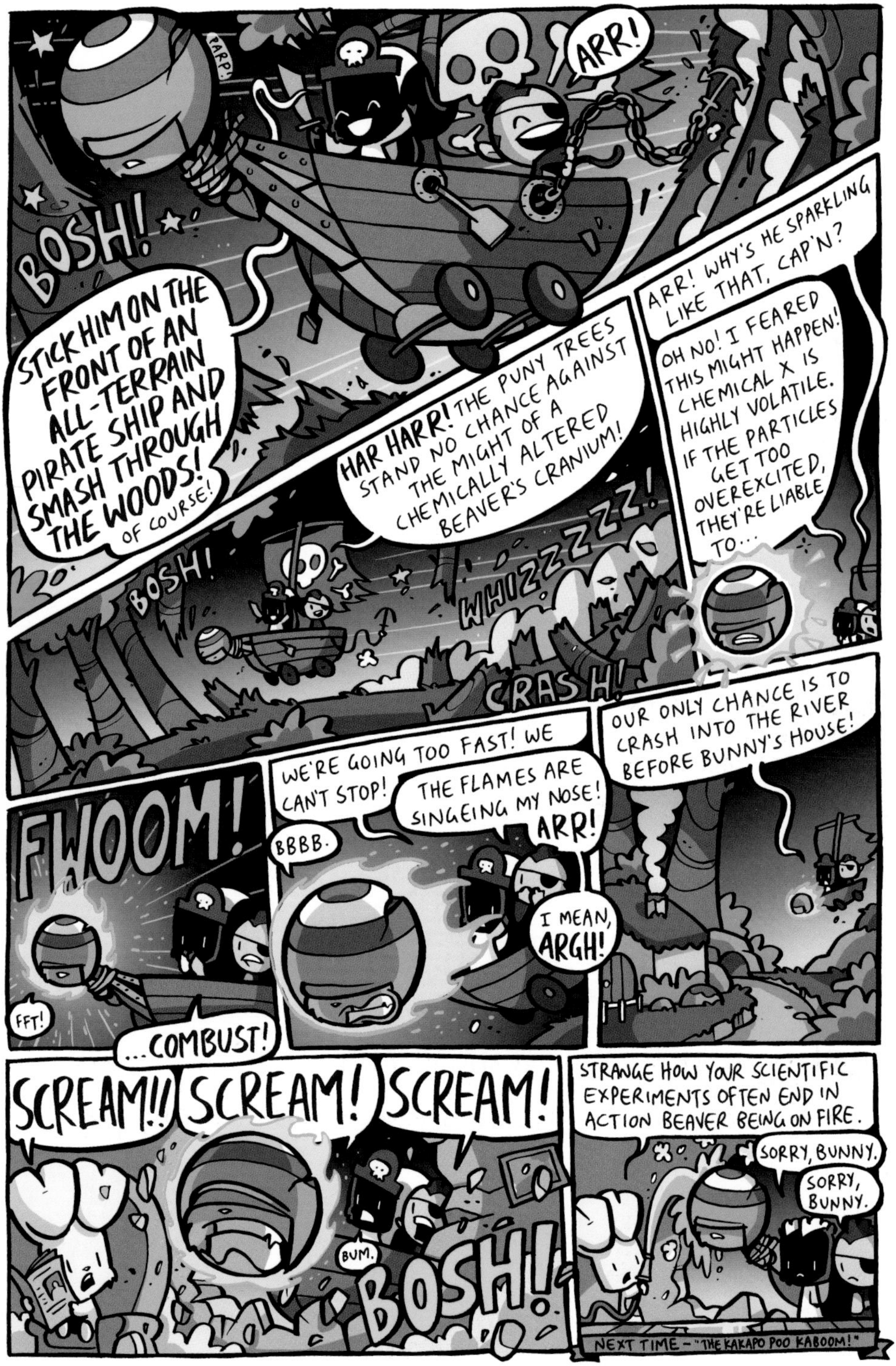
RARP.
ARR!
BOSH!
STICK HIM ON THE FRONT OF AN ALL-TERRAIN PIRATE SHIP AND SMASH THROUGH THE WOODS! OF COURSE!
HAR HARR! THE PUNY TREES STAND NO CHANCE AGAINST THE MIGHT OF A CHEMICALLY ALTERED BEAVER'S CRANIUM!
ARR! WHY'S HE SPARKLING LIKE THAT, CAP'N?
OH NO! I FEARED THIS MIGHT HAPPEN! CHEMICAL X IS HIGHLY VOLATILE. IF THE PARTICLES GET TOO OVEREXCITED, THEY'RE LIABLE TO...
BOSH!
WHIZZZZZZ!
CRASH!
FWOOM!
FFT!
...COMBUST!
WE'RE GOING TOO FAST! WE CAN'T STOP!
THE FLAMES ARE SINGEING MY NOSE! ARR!
BBBB.
I MEAN, ARGH!
OUR ONLY CHANCE IS TO CRASH INTO THE RIVER BEFORE BUNNY'S HOUSE!
SCREAM!! SCREAM! SCREAM!
BUM.
BOSH!
STRANGE HOW YOUR SCIENTIFIC EXPERIMENTS OFTEN END IN ACTION BEAVER BEING ON FIRE.
SORRY, BUNNY.
SORRY, BUNNY.
NEXT TIME - "THE KAKAPO POO KABOOM!"

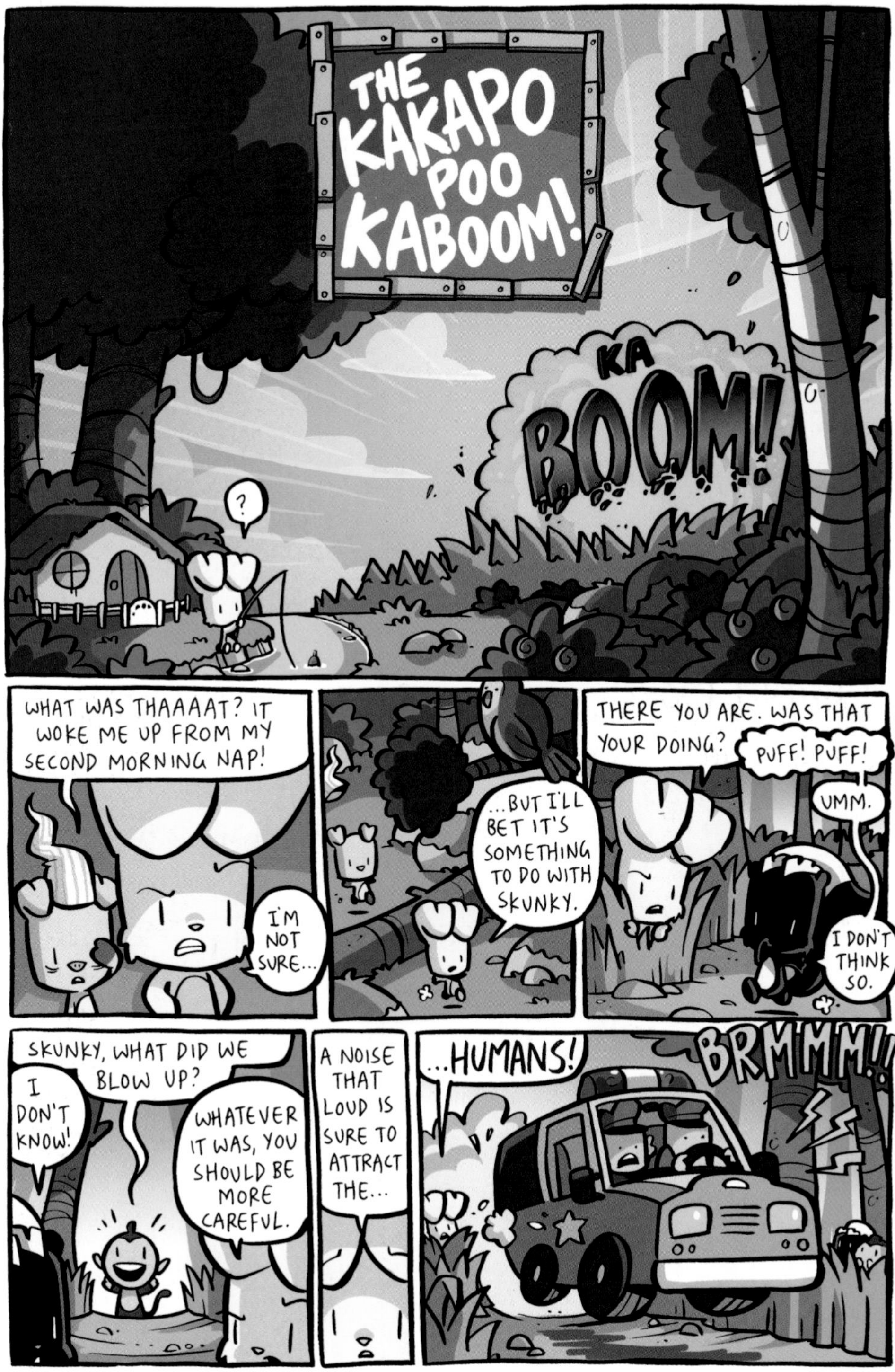
THE KAKAPO POO KABOOM!
KA BOOM!
?
WHAT WAS THAAAAT? IT WOKE ME UP FROM MY SECOND MORNING NAP!
I'M NOT SURE...
...BUT I'LL BET IT'S SOMETHING TO DO WITH SKUNKY.
THERE YOU ARE. WAS THAT YOUR DOING?
PUFF! PUFF!
UMM.
I DON'T THINK SO.
SKUNKY, WHAT DID WE BLOW UP?
I DON'T KNOW!
WHATEVER IT WAS, YOU SHOULD BE MORE CAREFUL.
A NOISE THAT LOUD IS SURE TO ATTRACT THE...
...HUMANS!
BRMMM!!!

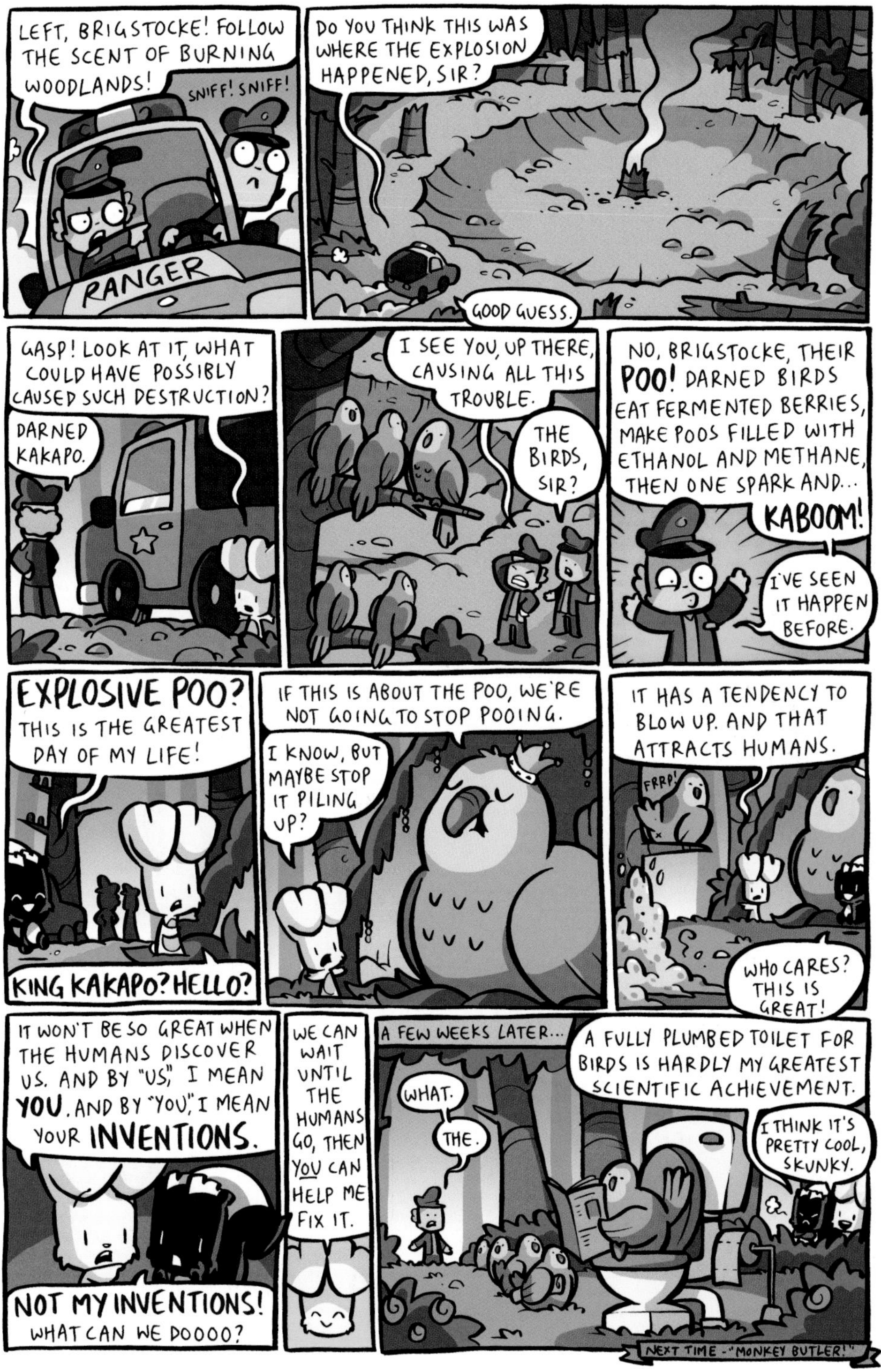
LEFT, BRIGSTOCKE! FOLLOW THE SCENT OF BURNING WOODLANDS!
SNIFF! SNIFF!
RANGER
DO YOU THINK THIS WAS WHERE THE EXPLOSION HAPPENED, SIR?
GOOD GUESS.
GASP! LOOK AT IT, WHAT COULD HAVE POSSIBLY CAUSED SUCH DESTRUCTION?
DARNED KAKAPO.
I SEE YOU, UP THERE, CAUSING ALL THIS TROUBLE.
THE BIRDS, SIR?
NO, BRIGSTOCKE, THEIR POO! DARNED BIRDS EAT FERMENTED BERRIES, MAKE POOS FILLED WITH ETHANOL AND METHANE, THEN ONE SPARK AND...
KABOOM!
I'VE SEEN IT HAPPEN BEFORE.
EXPLOSIVE POO? THIS IS THE GREATEST DAY OF MY LIFE!
KING KAKAPO? HELLO?
IF THIS IS ABOUT THE POO, WE'RE NOT GOING TO STOP POOING.
I KNOW, BUT MAYBE STOP IT PILING UP?
IT HAS A TENDENCY TO BLOW UP. AND THAT ATTRACTS HUMANS.
FRRP!
WHO CARES? THIS IS GREAT!
IT WON'T BE SO GREAT WHEN THE HUMANS DISCOVER US. AND BY "US," I MEAN YOU. AND BY "YOU," I MEAN YOUR INVENTIONS.
NOT MY INVENTIONS! WHAT CAN WE DOOOO?
WE CAN WAIT UNTIL THE HUMANS GO, THEN YOU CAN HELP ME FIX IT.
A FEW WEEKS LATER...
A FULLY PLUMBED TOILET FOR BIRDS IS HARDLY MY GREATEST SCIENTIFIC ACHIEVEMENT.
WHAT.
THE.
I THINK IT'S PRETTY COOL, SKUNKY.
NEXT TIME - "MONKEY BUTLER!"

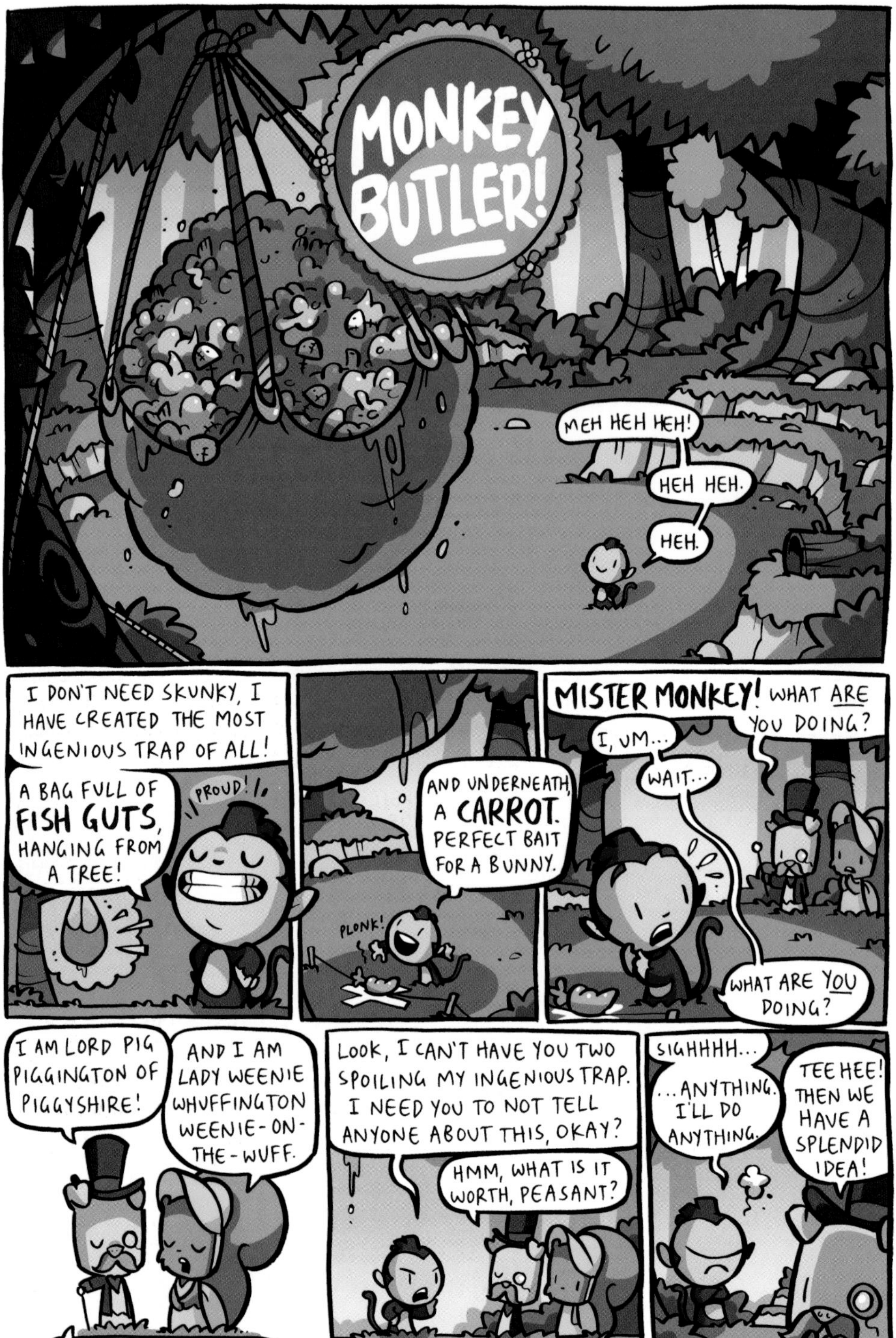
MONKEY BUTLER!
MEH HEH HEH!
HEH HEH.
HEH.
I DON'T NEED SKUNKY, I HAVE CREATED THE MOST INGENIOUS TRAP OF ALL!
A BAG FULL OF FISH GUTS, HANGING FROM A TREE!
PROUD!
AND UNDERNEATH, A CARROT. PERFECT BAIT FOR A BUNNY.
PLONK!
MISTER MONKEY! WHAT ARE YOU DOING?
I, UM...
WAIT...
WHAT ARE YOU DOING?
I AM LORD PIG PIGGINGTON OF PIGGYSHIRE!
AND I AM LADY WEENIE WHUFFINGTON WEENIE-ON-THE-WUFF.
WE ARE PLAYING FANCY!
LOOK, I CAN'T HAVE YOU TWO SPOILING MY INGENIOUS TRAP. I NEED YOU TO NOT TELL ANYONE ABOUT THIS, OKAY?
HMM, WHAT IS IT WORTH, PEASANT?
SIGHHHH...
...ANYTHING. I'LL DO ANYTHING.
TEE HEE! THEN WE HAVE A SPLENDID IDEA!

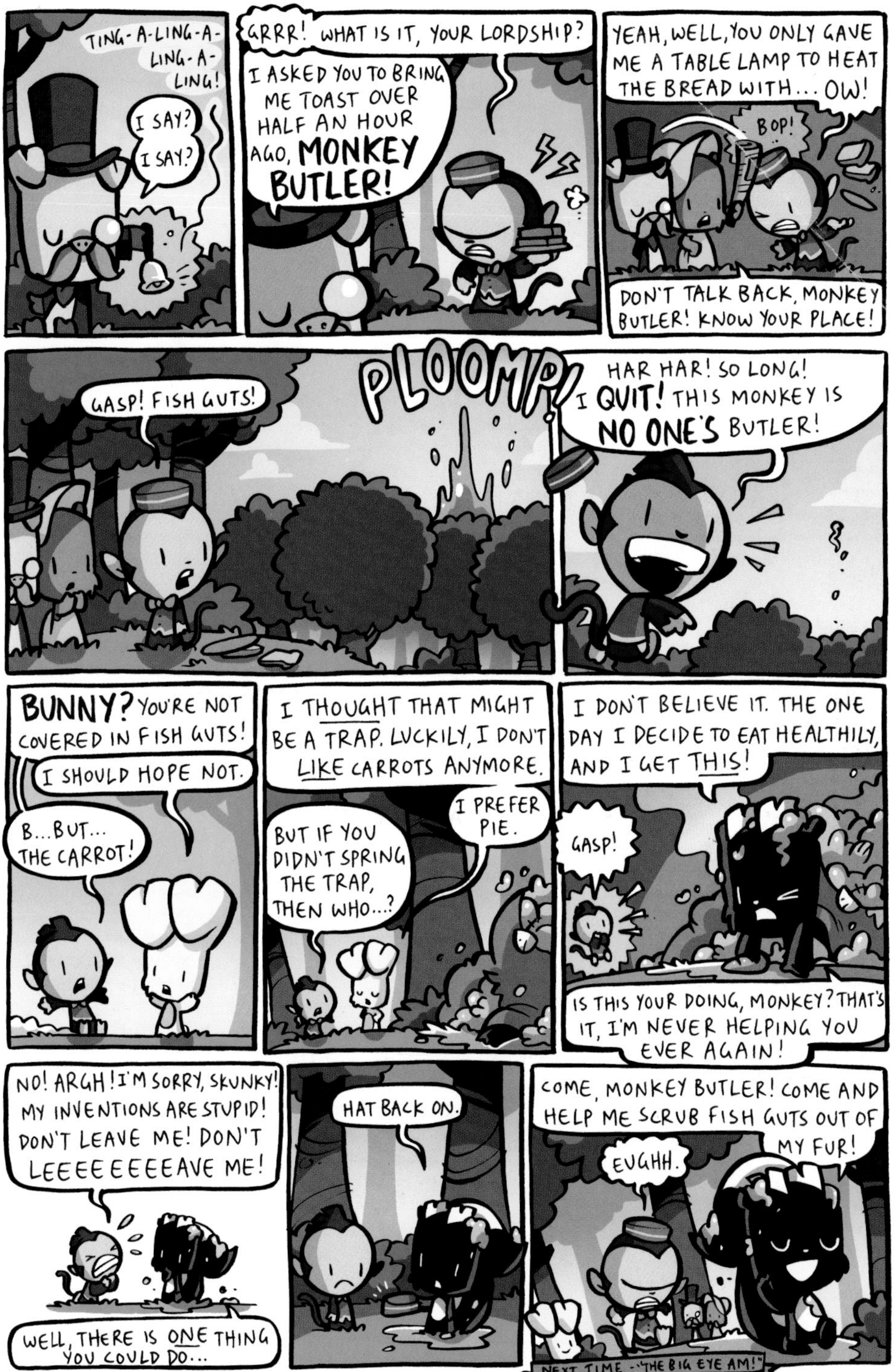
TING-A-LING-A-LING-A-LING!
I SAY?
I SAY?
GRRR! WHAT IS IT, YOUR LORDSHIP?
I ASKED YOU TO BRING ME TOAST OVER HALF AN HOUR AGO, MONKEY BUTLER!
YEAH, WELL, YOU ONLY GAVE ME A TABLE LAMP TO HEAT THE BREAD WITH... OW!
BOP!
DON'T TALK BACK, MONKEY BUTLER! KNOW YOUR PLACE!
GASP! FISH GUTS!
PLOOMP!
HAR HAR! SO LONG! I QUIT! THIS MONKEY IS NO ONE'S BUTLER!
BUNNY? YOU'RE NOT COVERED IN FISH GUTS!
I SHOULD HOPE NOT.
B...BUT... THE CARROT!
I THOUGHT THAT MIGHT BE A TRAP. LUCKILY, I DON'T LIKE CARROTS ANYMORE.
I PREFER PIE.
BUT IF YOU DIDN'T SPRING THE TRAP, THEN WHO...?
I DON'T BELIEVE IT. THE ONE DAY I DECIDE TO EAT HEALTHILY, AND I GET THIS!
GASP!
IS THIS YOUR DOING, MONKEY? THAT'S IT, I'M NEVER HELPING YOU EVER AGAIN!
NO! ARGH! I'M SORRY, SKUNKY! MY INVENTIONS ARE STUPID! DON'T LEAVE ME! DON'T LEEEEEEEEAVE ME!
WELL, THERE IS ONE THING YOU COULD DO...
HAT BACK ON.
COME, MONKEY BUTLER! COME AND HELP ME SCRUB FISH GUTS OUT OF MY FUR!
EUGHH.
NEXT TIME - "THE BIG EYE AM!"

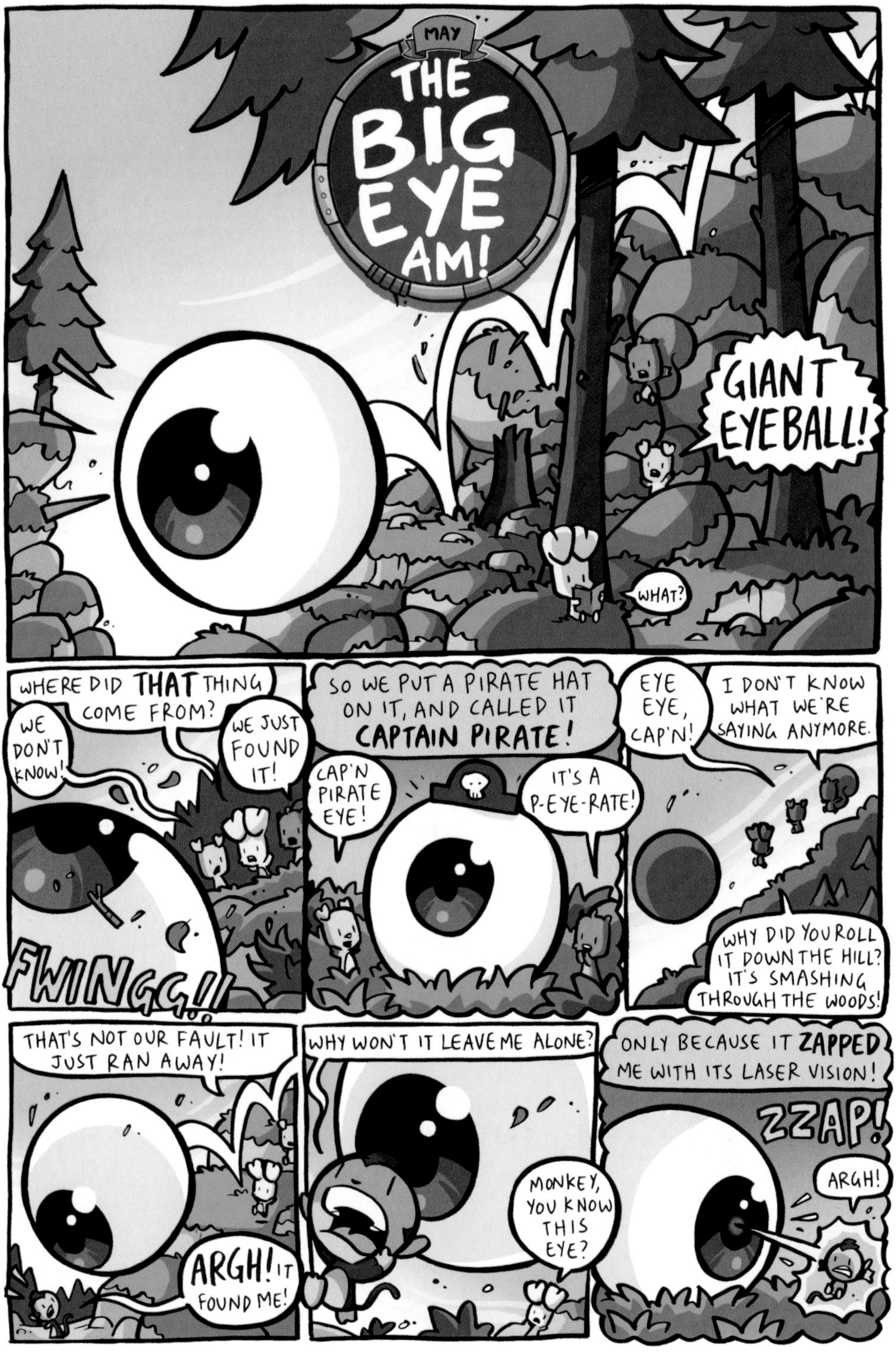
MAY
THE BIG EYE AM!
GIANT EYEBALL!
WHAT?
WHERE DID THAT THING COME FROM?
WE DON'T KNOW!
WE JUST FOUND IT!
FWINGG!!
SO WE PUT A PIRATE HAT ON IT, AND CALLED IT CAPTAIN PIRATE!
CAP'N PIRATE EYE!
IT'S A P-EYE-RATE!
EYE EYE, CAP'N!
I DON'T KNOW WHAT WE'RE SAYING ANYMORE.
WHY DID YOU ROLL IT DOWN THE HILL? IT'S SMASHING THROUGH THE WOODS!
THAT'S NOT OUR FAULT! IT JUST RAN AWAY!
ARGH! IT FOUND ME!
WHY WON'T IT LEAVE ME ALONE?
MONKEY, YOU KNOW THIS EYE?
ONLY BECAUSE IT ZAPPED ME WITH ITS LASER VISION!
ZZAP!
ARGH!

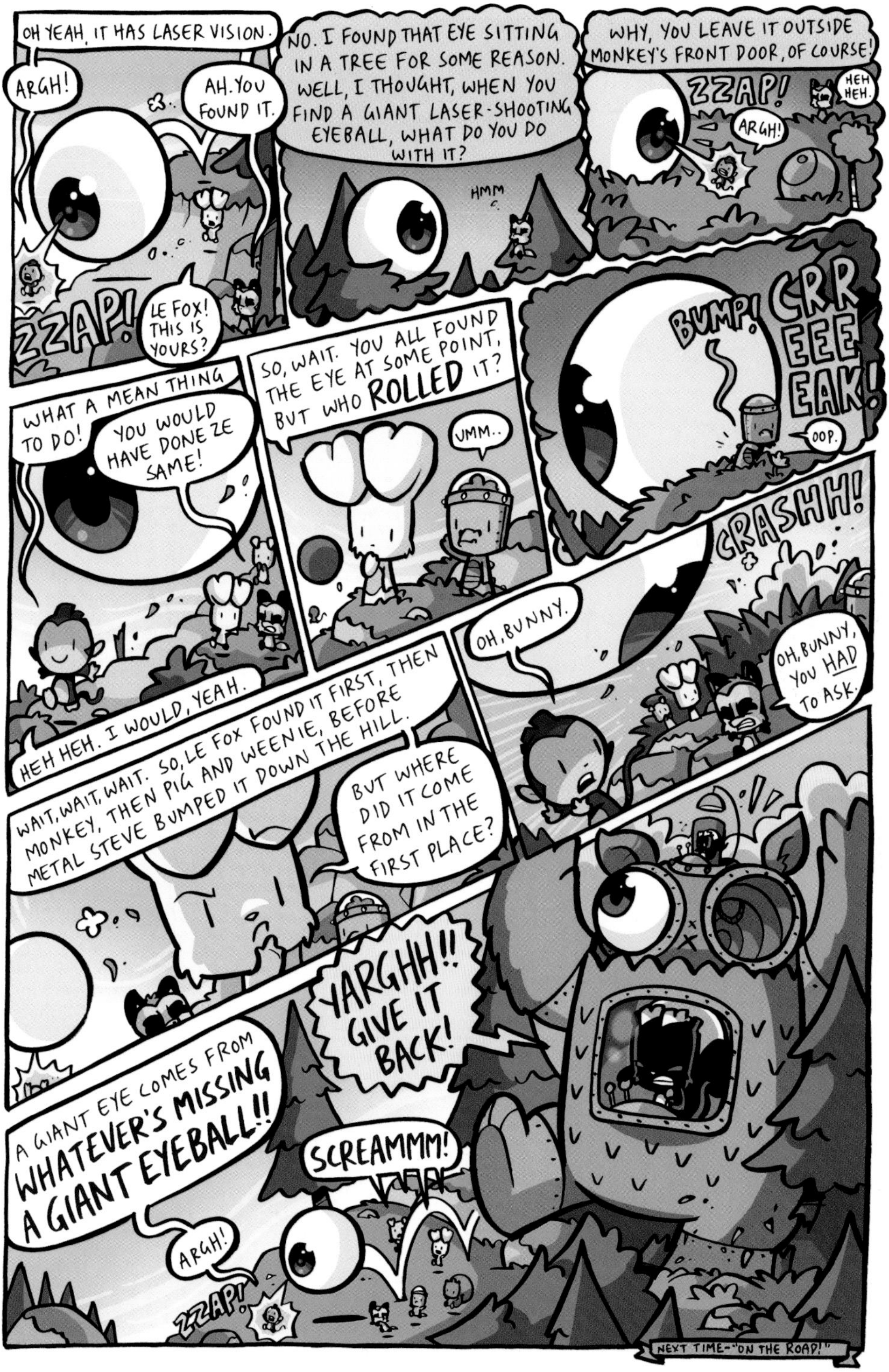
OH YEAH, IT HAS LASER VISION.
ARGH!
AH. YOU FOUND IT.
ZZAP!
LE FOX! THIS IS YOURS?
NO. I FOUND THAT EYE SITTING IN A TREE FOR SOME REASON. WELL, I THOUGHT, WHEN YOU FIND A GIANT LASER-SHOOTING EYEBALL, WHAT DO YOU DO WITH IT?
HMM
WHY, YOU LEAVE IT OUTSIDE MONKEY'S FRONT DOOR, OF COURSE!
ZZAP!
HEH HEH.
ARGH!
WHAT A MEAN THING TO DO!
YOU WOULD HAVE DONE ZE SAME!
SO, WAIT. YOU ALL FOUND THE EYE AT SOME POINT, BUT WHO **ROLLED** IT?
UMM..
BUMP!
CRR EEE EAK!
OOP.
HEH HEH. I WOULD, YEAH.
CRASHH!
OH, BUNNY.
OH, BUNNY, YOU HAD TO ASK.
WAIT, WAIT, WAIT. SO, LE FOX FOUND IT FIRST, THEN MONKEY, THEN PIG AND WEENIE, BEFORE METAL STEVE BUMPED IT DOWN THE HILL.
BUT WHERE DID IT COME FROM IN THE FIRST PLACE?
YARGHH!! GIVE IT BACK!
A GIANT EYE COMES FROM **WHATEVER'S MISSING A GIANT EYEBALL!!**
SCREAMMM!
ARGH!
ZZAP!
NEXT TIME—"ON THE ROAD!"

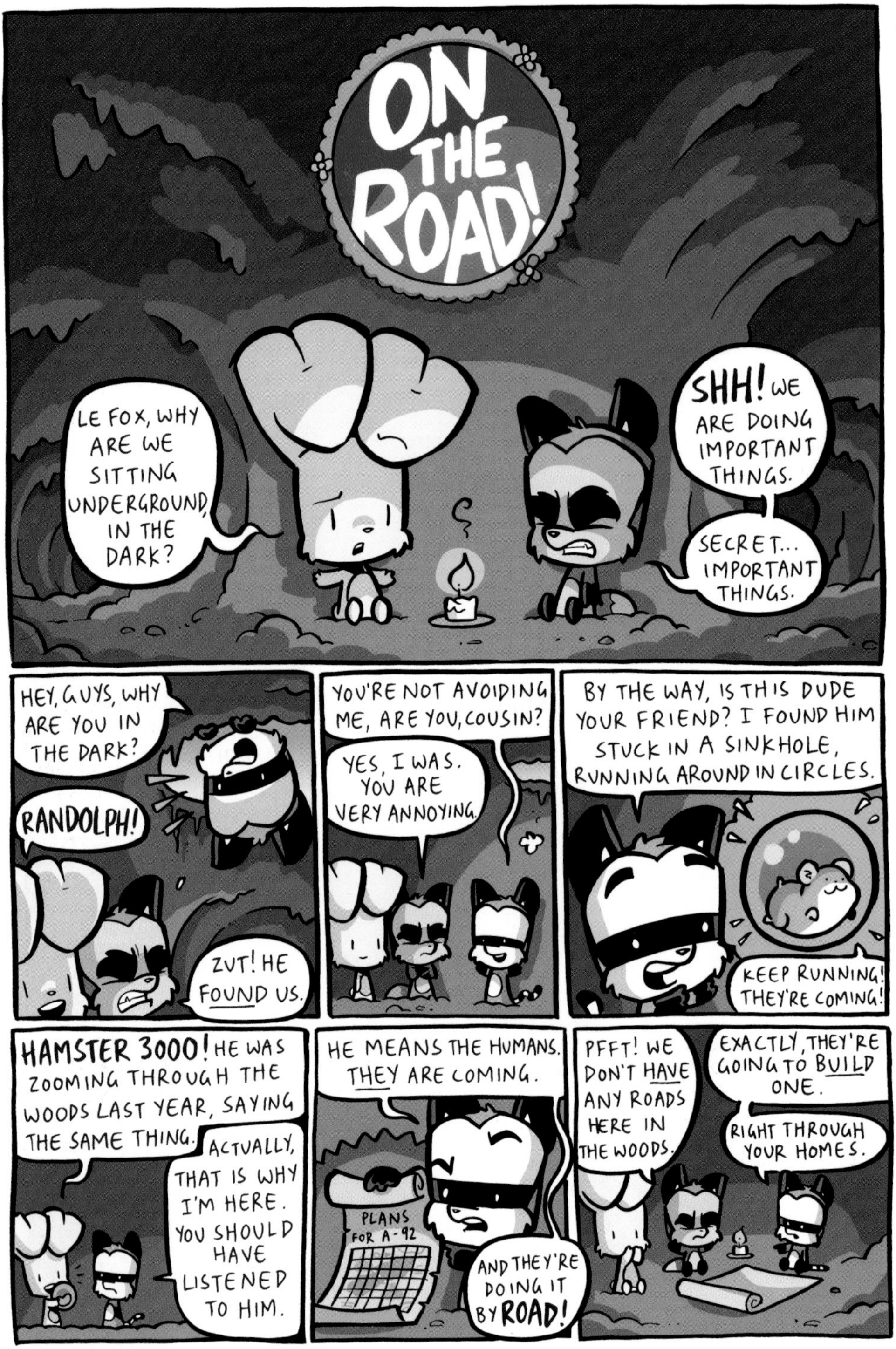
ON THE ROAD!
LE FOX, WHY ARE WE SITTING UNDERGROUND, IN THE DARK?
SHH! WE ARE DOING IMPORTANT THINGS.
SECRET... IMPORTANT THINGS.
HEY, GUYS, WHY ARE YOU IN THE DARK?
RANDOLPH!
ZUT! HE FOUND US.
YOU'RE NOT AVOIDING ME, ARE YOU, COUSIN?
YES, I WAS. YOU ARE VERY ANNOYING.
BY THE WAY, IS THIS DUDE YOUR FRIEND? I FOUND HIM STUCK IN A SINKHOLE, RUNNING AROUND IN CIRCLES.
KEEP RUNNING! THEY'RE COMING!
HAMSTER 3000! HE WAS ZOOMING THROUGH THE WOODS LAST YEAR, SAYING THE SAME THING.
ACTUALLY, THAT IS WHY I'M HERE. YOU SHOULD HAVE LISTENED TO HIM.
HE MEANS THE HUMANS. THEY ARE COMING.
PLANS FOR A-92
AND THEY'RE DOING IT BY ROAD!
PFFT! WE DON'T HAVE ANY ROADS HERE IN THE WOODS.
EXACTLY, THEY'RE GOING TO BUILD ONE.
RIGHT THROUGH YOUR HOMES.

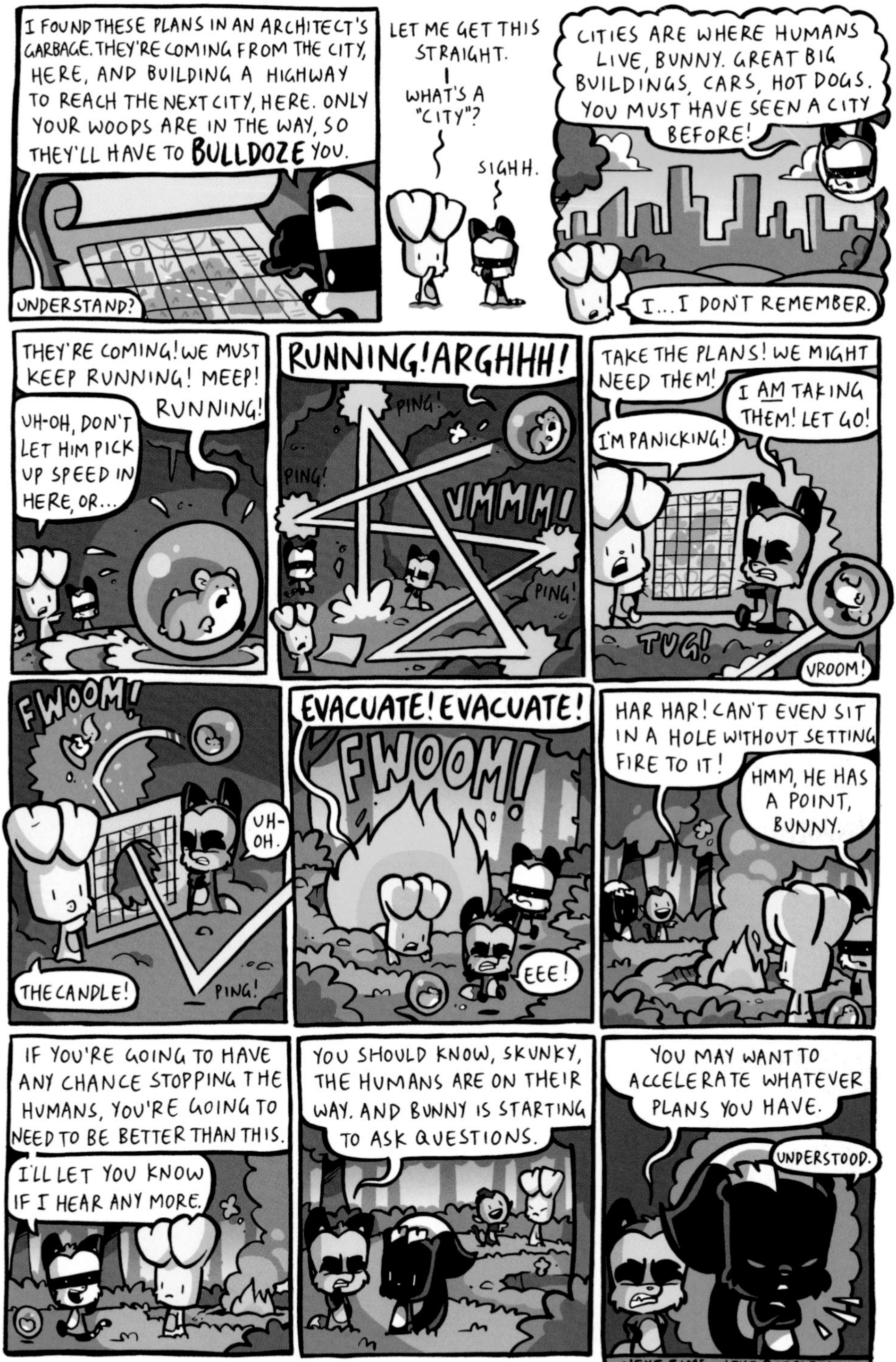
I FOUND THESE PLANS IN AN ARCHITECT'S GARBAGE. THEY'RE COMING FROM THE CITY, HERE, AND BUILDING A HIGHWAY TO REACH THE NEXT CITY, HERE. ONLY YOUR WOODS ARE IN THE WAY, SO THEY'LL HAVE TO BULLDOZE YOU.
UNDERSTAND?
LET ME GET THIS STRAIGHT.
WHAT'S A "CITY"?
SIGHH.
CITIES ARE WHERE HUMANS LIVE, BUNNY. GREAT BIG BUILDINGS, CARS, HOT DOGS. YOU MUST HAVE SEEN A CITY BEFORE!
I... I DON'T REMEMBER.
THEY'RE COMING! WE MUST KEEP RUNNING! MEEP!
RUNNING!
UH-OH, DON'T LET HIM PICK UP SPEED IN HERE, OR...
RUNNING! ARGHHH!
PING!
PING!
VMMM!
PING!
TAKE THE PLANS! WE MIGHT NEED THEM!
I AM TAKING THEM! LET GO!
I'M PANICKING!
TUG!
VROOM!
FWOOM!
UH-OH.
THE CANDLE!
PING!
EVACUATE! EVACUATE!
FWOOM!
EEE!
HAR HAR! CAN'T EVEN SIT IN A HOLE WITHOUT SETTING FIRE TO IT!
HMM, HE HAS A POINT, BUNNY.
IF YOU'RE GOING TO HAVE ANY CHANCE STOPPING THE HUMANS, YOU'RE GOING TO NEED TO BE BETTER THAN THIS.
I'LL LET YOU KNOW IF I HEAR ANY MORE.
YOU SHOULD KNOW, SKUNKY, THE HUMANS ARE ON THEIR WAY. AND BUNNY IS STARTING TO ASK QUESTIONS.
YOU MAY WANT TO ACCELERATE WHATEVER PLANS YOU HAVE.
UNDERSTOOD.
NEXT TIME - "THE PURPLE!"

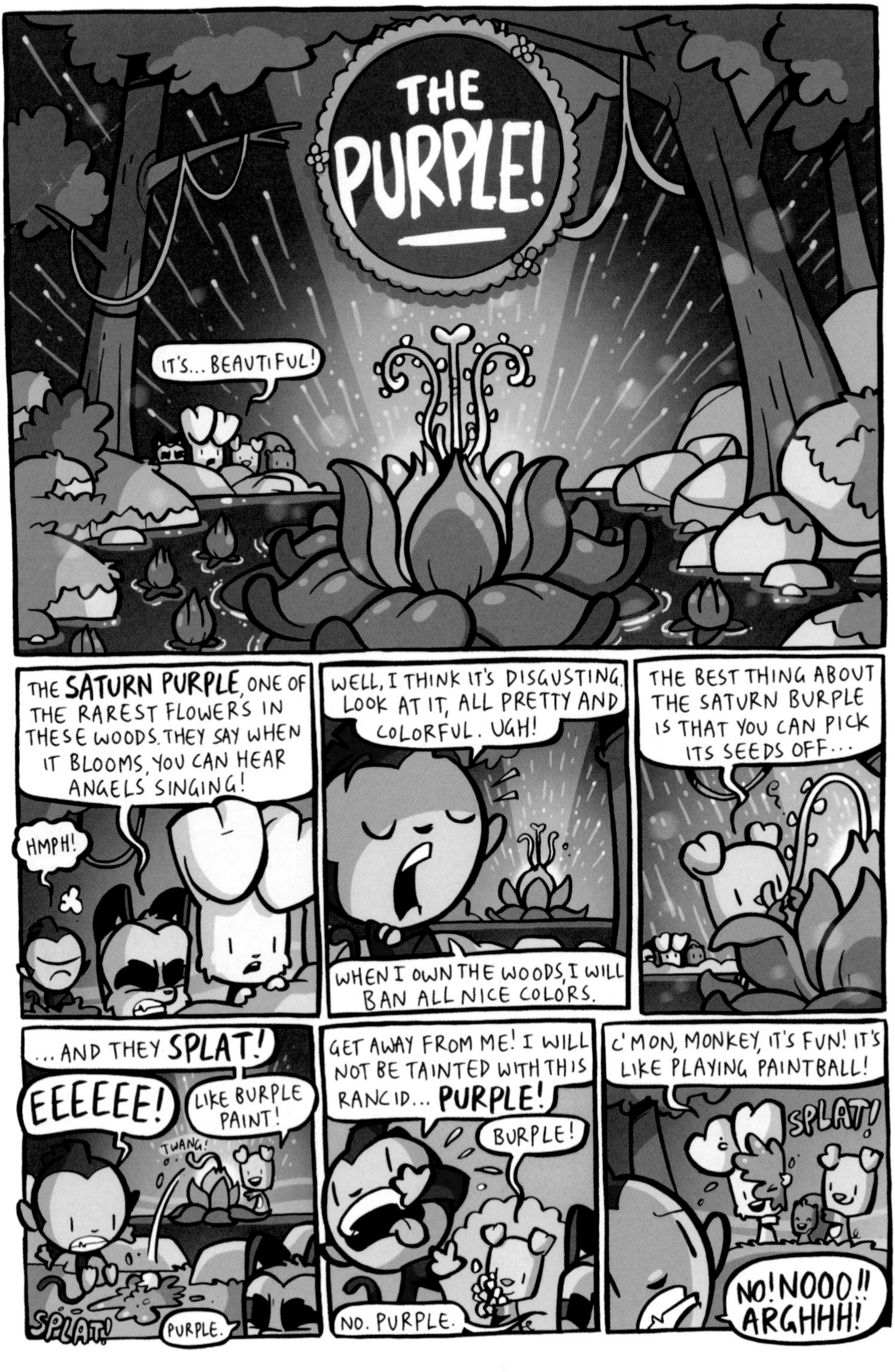
THE PURPLE!
IT'S... BEAUTIFUL!
THE SATURN PURPLE, ONE OF THE RAREST FLOWERS IN THESE WOODS. THEY SAY WHEN IT BLOOMS, YOU CAN HEAR ANGELS SINGING!
HMPH!
WELL, I THINK IT'S DISGUSTING. LOOK AT IT, ALL PRETTY AND COLORFUL. UGH!
WHEN I OWN THE WOODS, I WILL BAN ALL NICE COLORS.
THE BEST THING ABOUT THE SATURN BURPLE IS THAT YOU CAN PICK ITS SEEDS OFF...
...AND THEY SPLAT!
EEEEEE!
LIKE BURPLE PAINT!
TWANG!
SPLAT!
PURPLE.
GET AWAY FROM ME! I WILL NOT BE TAINTED WITH THIS RANCID... PURPLE!
BURPLE!
NO. PURPLE.
C'MON, MONKEY, IT'S FUN! IT'S LIKE PLAYING PAINTBALL!
SPLAT!
NO! NOOO!! ARGHHH!

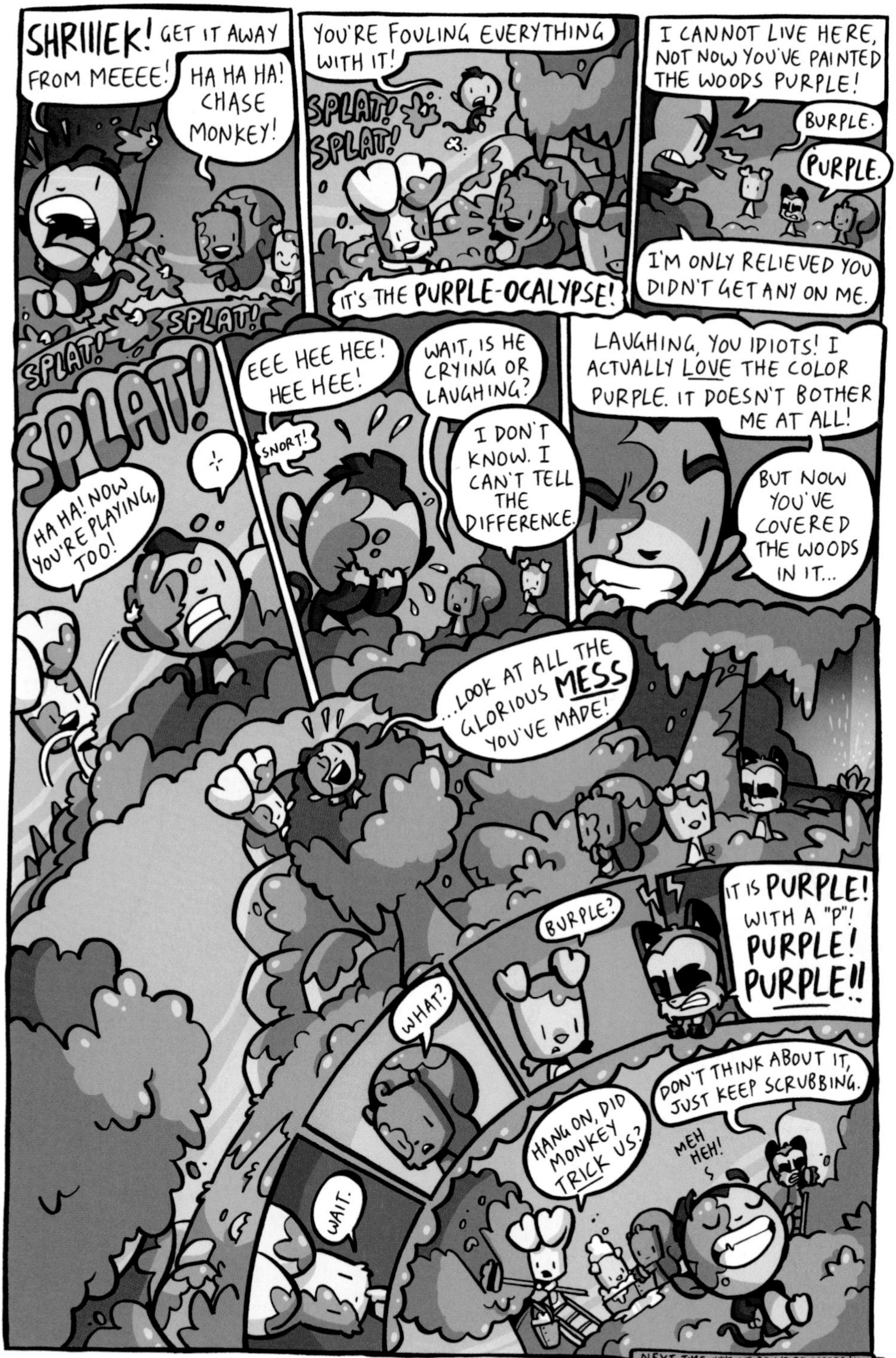
SHRIIIEK! GET IT AWAY FROM MEEEE!
HA HA HA! CHASE MONKEY!
YOU'RE FOULING EVERYTHING WITH IT!
SPLAT! SPLAT!
IT'S THE PURPLE-OCALYPSE!
I CANNOT LIVE HERE, NOT NOW YOU'VE PAINTED THE WOODS PURPLE!
BURPLE.
PURPLE.
I'M ONLY RELIEVED YOU DIDN'T GET ANY ON ME.
SPLAT! SPLAT!
SPLAT!
HA HA! NOW YOU'RE PLAYING, TOO!
EEE HEE HEE! HEE HEE!
SNORT!
WAIT, IS HE CRYING OR LAUGHING?
I DON'T KNOW. I CAN'T TELL THE DIFFERENCE.
LAUGHING, YOU IDIOTS! I ACTUALLY LOVE THE COLOR PURPLE. IT DOESN'T BOTHER ME AT ALL!
BUT NOW YOU'VE COVERED THE WOODS IN IT...
...LOOK AT ALL THE GLORIOUS MESS YOU'VE MADE!
BURPLE?
IT IS PURPLE! WITH A "P"! PURPLE! PURPLE!!
WHAT?
WAIT.
HANG ON, DID MONKEY TRICK US?
DON'T THINK ABOUT IT, JUST KEEP SCRUBBING.
MEH HEH!
NEXT TIME - "THE WEIRD, WEIRD WOODS!"

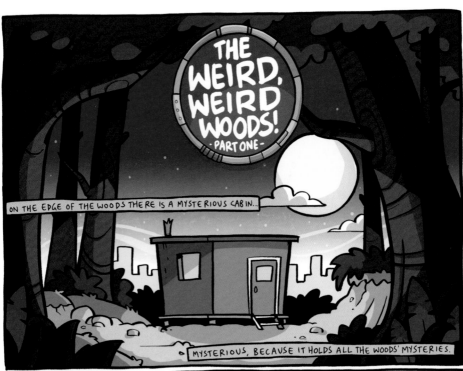

THE WEIRD, WEIRD WOODS!
-PART ONE-

ON THE EDGE OF THE WOODS THERE IS A MYSTERIOUS CABIN...

MYSTERIOUS, BECAUSE IT HOLDS ALL THE WOODS' MYSTERIES.

TINK A TINK A TINK

WORLD'S #1 RANGER

NOW. WHERE WERE WE?

THE WEIRD WOODS WALL

AND ONE MAN IS DETERMINED TO FIGURE THEM OUT.

PHEW! SURE IS DARK OUT THERE. FELT LIKE SOMETHING WAS WATCHING ME, TOO.

PROBABLY WAS!

YOU'RE NOT LOOKING AT YOUR WEIRD WOODS WALL AGAIN, ARE YOU? LET IT GO.

BUT THERE ARE TOO MANY STRANGE THINGS GOING ON!

MASSIVE EXPLOSIONS! CLANKING MACHINERY! DISTANT GIGGLING, MANIACAL LAUGHING, AND CRAZY SCREAMING!

NOT TO MENTION THE THINGS WE'VE FOUND.

46

THAT GIANT EYEBALL EMBEDDED IN THE MIDDLE OF THE ROAD!

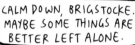

THE WEIRD, SPIKY SKIN THAT BLEW INTO TOWN.

OR HOW ABOUT **THE HEAD OF AN ENORMOUS CHICKEN-SHAPED ZEPPELIN!?**

CLUCK!

SOMETHING'S GOING ON!

CALM DOWN, BRIGSTOCKE. MAYBE SOME THINGS ARE BETTER LEFT ALONE.

YOU! YOU KNOW WHAT'S GOING ON, DON'T YOU!

TELL ME...

CREEEEAKK!

DID YOU HEAR SOMETHING?

YOU LEFT THE DOOR OPEN!

IT'S COMING INSIDE!

HOLD ME!

HOLD ME!

CREAKK!

WE'RE RAIDING YOUR FORT!! BLOO BLOO BLOO BLOO!!

BLOO.

SCREAM! SCREAM!

PERHAPS SOME MYSTERIES WILL NEVER BE ANSWERED...

WHY WAS THAT PIG DRESSED LIKE THAT?

OR MAYBE THEY WILL, IN PART TWO — NEXT TIME!!

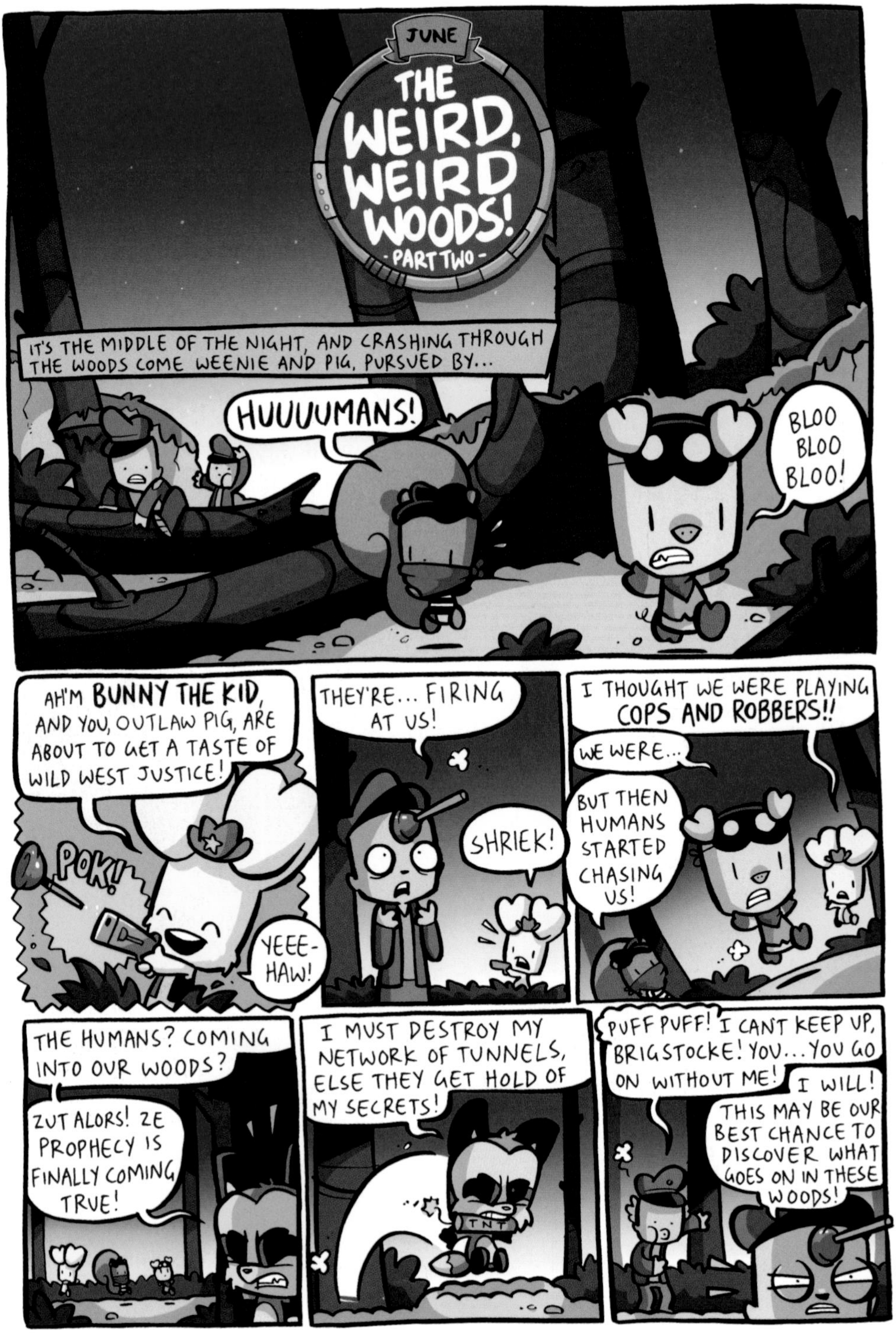
JUNE
THE WEIRD, WEIRD WOODS!
- PART TWO -
IT'S THE MIDDLE OF THE NIGHT, AND CRASHING THROUGH THE WOODS COME WEENIE AND PIG, PURSUED BY...
HUUUUMANS!
BLOO BLOO BLOO!
AH'M BUNNY THE KID, AND YOU, OUTLAW PIG, ARE ABOUT TO GET A TASTE OF WILD WEST JUSTICE!
POK!
YEEE-HAW!
THEY'RE... FIRING AT US!
SHRIEK!
I THOUGHT WE WERE PLAYING COPS AND ROBBERS!!
WE WERE...
BUT THEN HUMANS STARTED CHASING US!
THE HUMANS? COMING INTO OUR WOODS?
ZUT ALORS! ZE PROPHECY IS FINALLY COMING TRUE!
I MUST DESTROY MY NETWORK OF TUNNELS, ELSE THEY GET HOLD OF MY SECRETS!
TNT
PUFF PUFF! I CAN'T KEEP UP, BRIGSTOCKE! YOU... YOU GO ON WITHOUT ME!
I WILL! THIS MAY BE OUR BEST CHANCE TO DISCOVER WHAT GOES ON IN THESE WOODS!

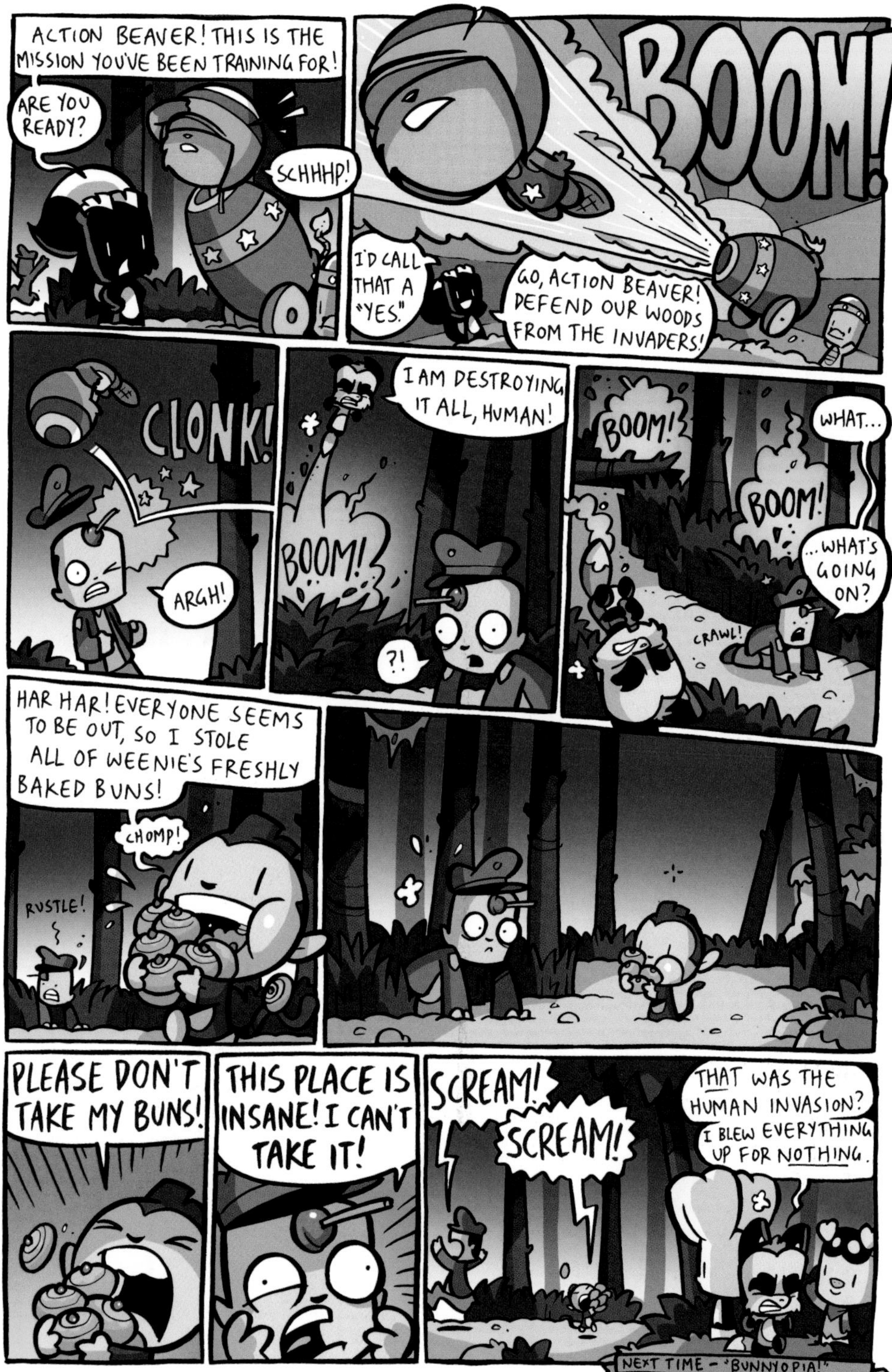
ACTION BEAVER! THIS IS THE MISSION YOU'VE BEEN TRAINING FOR!
ARE YOU READY?
SCHHHP!
BOOM!
I'D CALL THAT A "YES."
GO, ACTION BEAVER! DEFEND OUR WOODS FROM THE INVADERS!
CLONK!
ARGH!
I AM DESTROYING IT ALL, HUMAN!
BOOM!
?!
BOOM!
WHAT...
BOOM!
...WHAT'S GOING ON?
CRAWL!
HAR HAR! EVERYONE SEEMS TO BE OUT, SO I STOLE ALL OF WEENIE'S FRESHLY BAKED BUNS!
CHOMP!
RUSTLE!
PLEASE DON'T TAKE MY BUNS!
THIS PLACE IS INSANE! I CAN'T TAKE IT!
SCREAM!
SCREAM!
THAT WAS THE HUMAN INVASION? I BLEW EVERYTHING UP FOR NOTHING.
NEXT TIME - "BUNNYOPIA!"

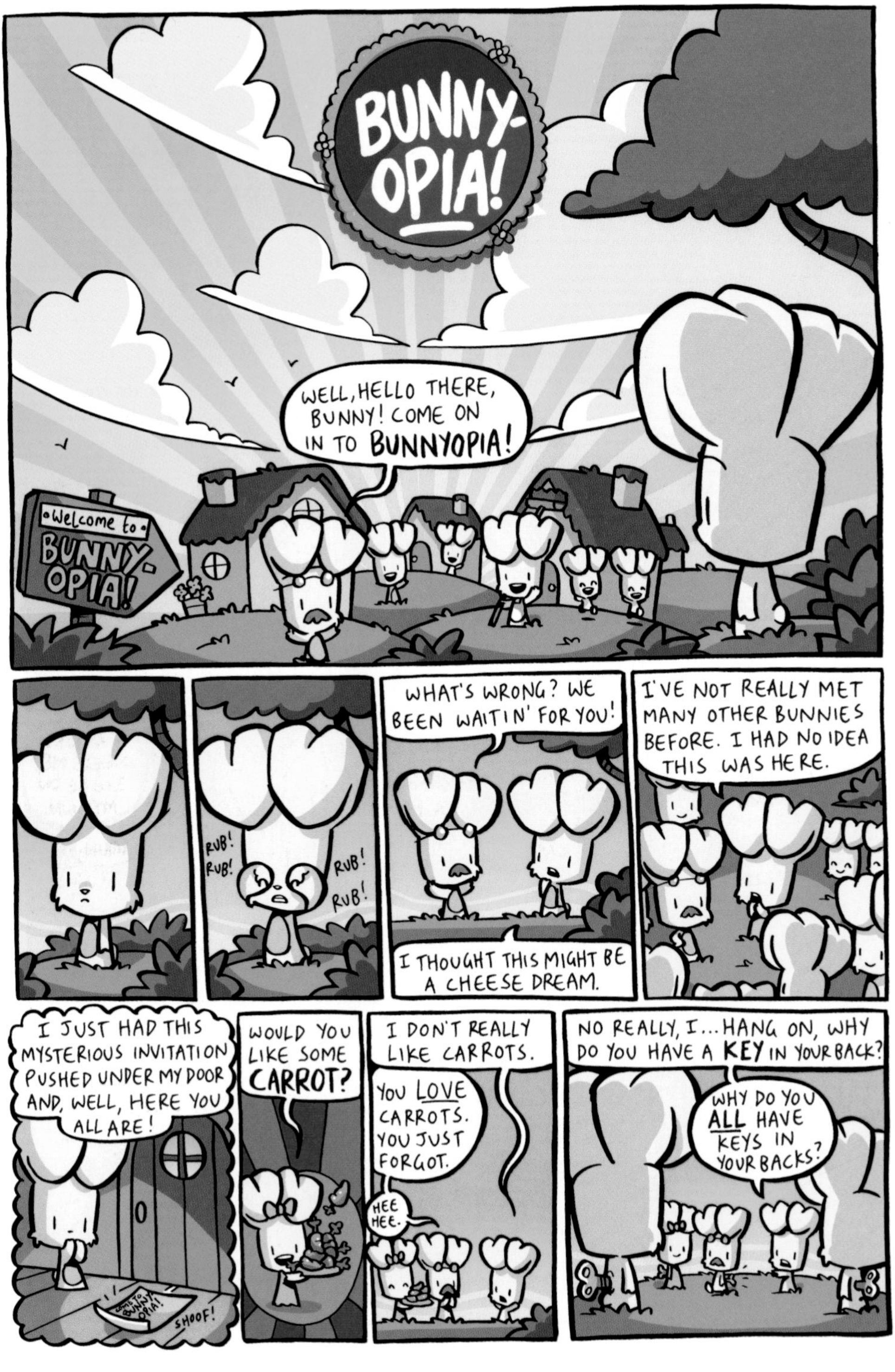
BUNNY-OPIA!
WELL, HELLO THERE, BUNNY! COME ON IN TO BUNNYOPIA!
Welcome to BUNNY-OPIA!
RUB! RUB!
RUB! RUB!
WHAT'S WRONG? WE BEEN WAITIN' FOR YOU!
I THOUGHT THIS MIGHT BE A CHEESE DREAM.
I'VE NOT REALLY MET MANY OTHER BUNNIES BEFORE. I HAD NO IDEA THIS WAS HERE.
I JUST HAD THIS MYSTERIOUS INVITATION PUSHED UNDER MY DOOR AND, WELL, HERE YOU ALL ARE!
SHOOF!
WOULD YOU LIKE SOME CARROT?
I DON'T REALLY LIKE CARROTS.
YOU LOVE CARROTS. YOU JUST FORGOT.
HEE HEE.
NO REALLY, I... HANG ON, WHY DO YOU HAVE A KEY IN YOUR BACK?
WHY DO YOU ALL HAVE KEYS IN YOUR BACKS?

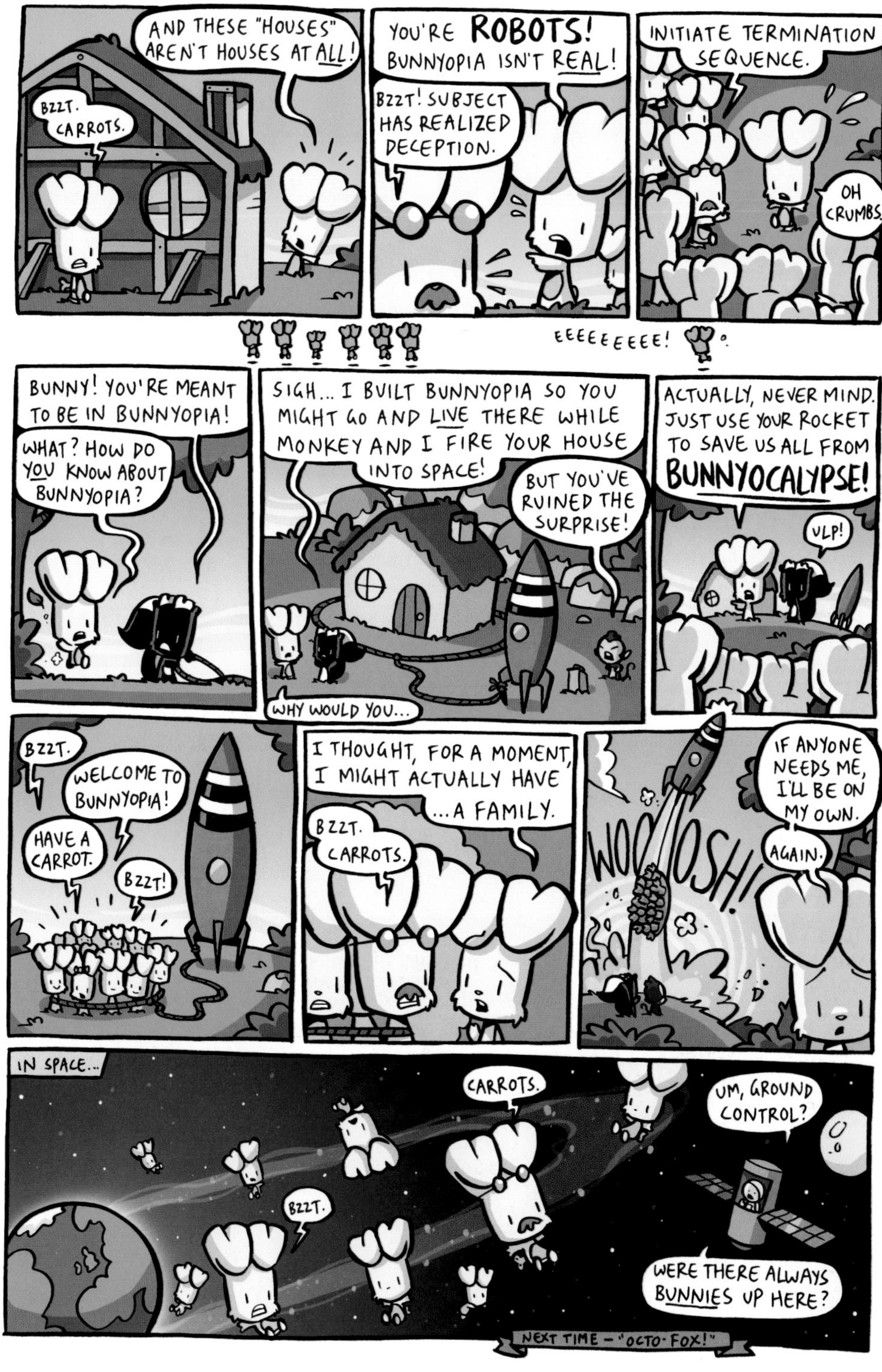
AND THESE "HOUSES" AREN'T HOUSES AT ALL!
BZZT. CARROTS.
YOU'RE ROBOTS! BUNNYOPIA ISN'T REAL!
BZZT! SUBJECT HAS REALIZED DECEPTION.
INITIATE TERMINATION SEQUENCE.
OH CRUMBS.
EEEEEEEEE!
BUNNY! YOU'RE MEANT TO BE IN BUNNYOPIA!
WHAT? HOW DO YOU KNOW ABOUT BUNNYOPIA?
SIGH... I BUILT BUNNYOPIA SO YOU MIGHT GO AND LIVE THERE WHILE MONKEY AND I FIRE YOUR HOUSE INTO SPACE!
BUT YOU'VE RUINED THE SURPRISE!
WHY WOULD YOU...
ACTUALLY, NEVER MIND. JUST USE YOUR ROCKET TO SAVE US ALL FROM BUNNYOCALYPSE!
ULP!
BZZT.
WELCOME TO BUNNYOPIA!
HAVE A CARROT.
BZZT!
I THOUGHT, FOR A MOMENT, I MIGHT ACTUALLY HAVE ...A FAMILY.
BZZT. CARROTS.
WOOOSH!
IF ANYONE NEEDS ME, I'LL BE ON MY OWN.
AGAIN.
IN SPACE...
CARROTS.
UM, GROUND CONTROL?
BZZT.
WERE THERE ALWAYS BUNNIES UP HERE?
NEXT TIME – "OCTO-FOX!"

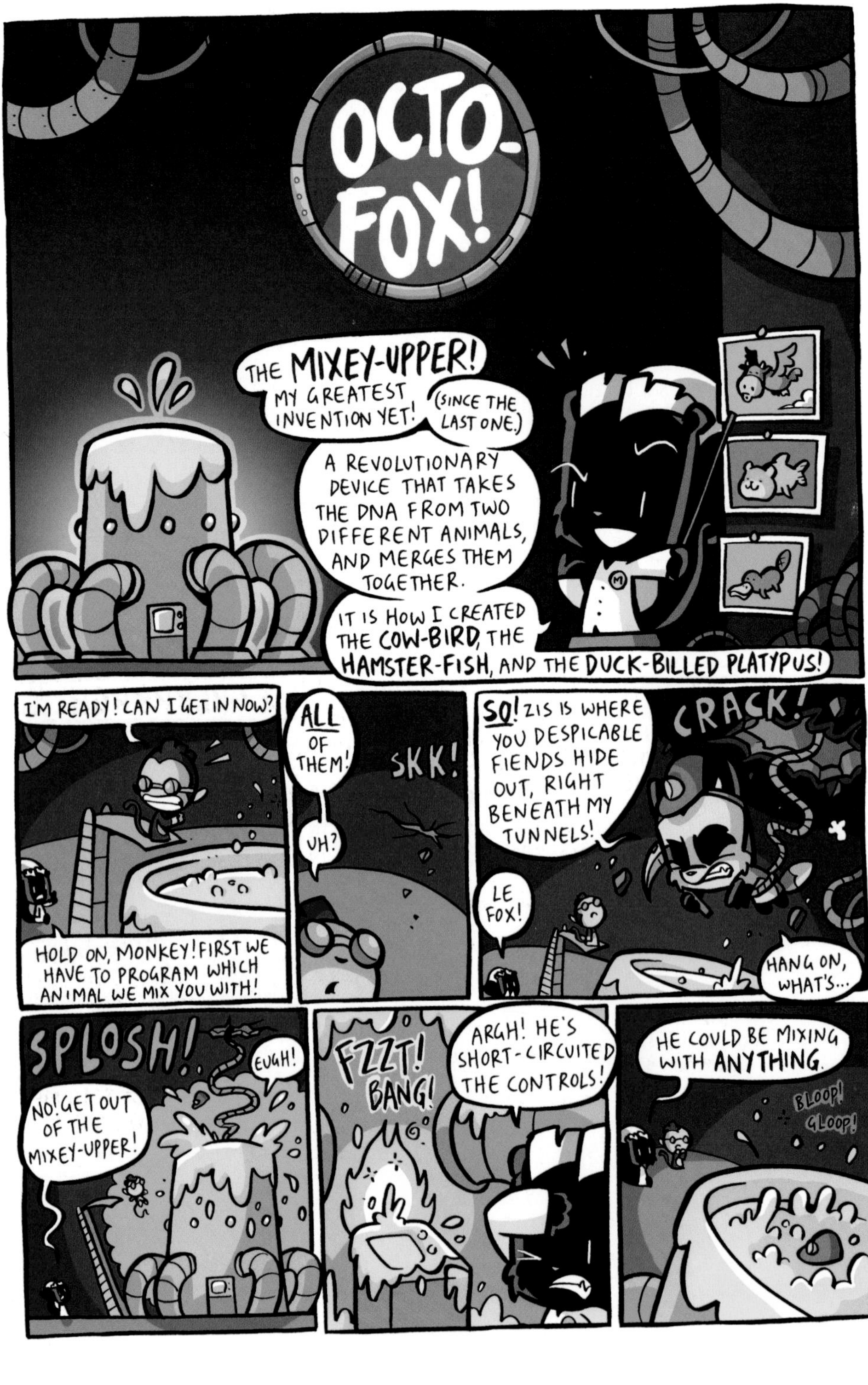
OCTO-FOX!
THE MIXEY-UPPER! MY GREATEST INVENTION YET!
(SINCE THE LAST ONE.)
A REVOLUTIONARY DEVICE THAT TAKES THE DNA FROM TWO DIFFERENT ANIMALS, AND MERGES THEM TOGETHER.
IT IS HOW I CREATED THE COW-BIRD, THE HAMSTER-FISH, AND THE DUCK-BILLED PLATYPUS!
I'M READY! CAN I GET IN NOW?
HOLD ON, MONKEY! FIRST WE HAVE TO PROGRAM WHICH ANIMAL WE MIX YOU WITH!
ALL OF THEM!
SKK!
UH?
SO! ZIS IS WHERE YOU DESPICABLE FIENDS HIDE OUT, RIGHT BENEATH MY TUNNELS!
CRACK!
LE FOX!
HANG ON, WHAT'S...
SPLOSH!
EUGH!
NO! GET OUT OF THE MIXEY-UPPER!
FZZT! BANG!
ARGH! HE'S SHORT-CIRCUITED THE CONTROLS!
HE COULD BE MIXING WITH ANYTHING.
BLOOP! GLOOP!

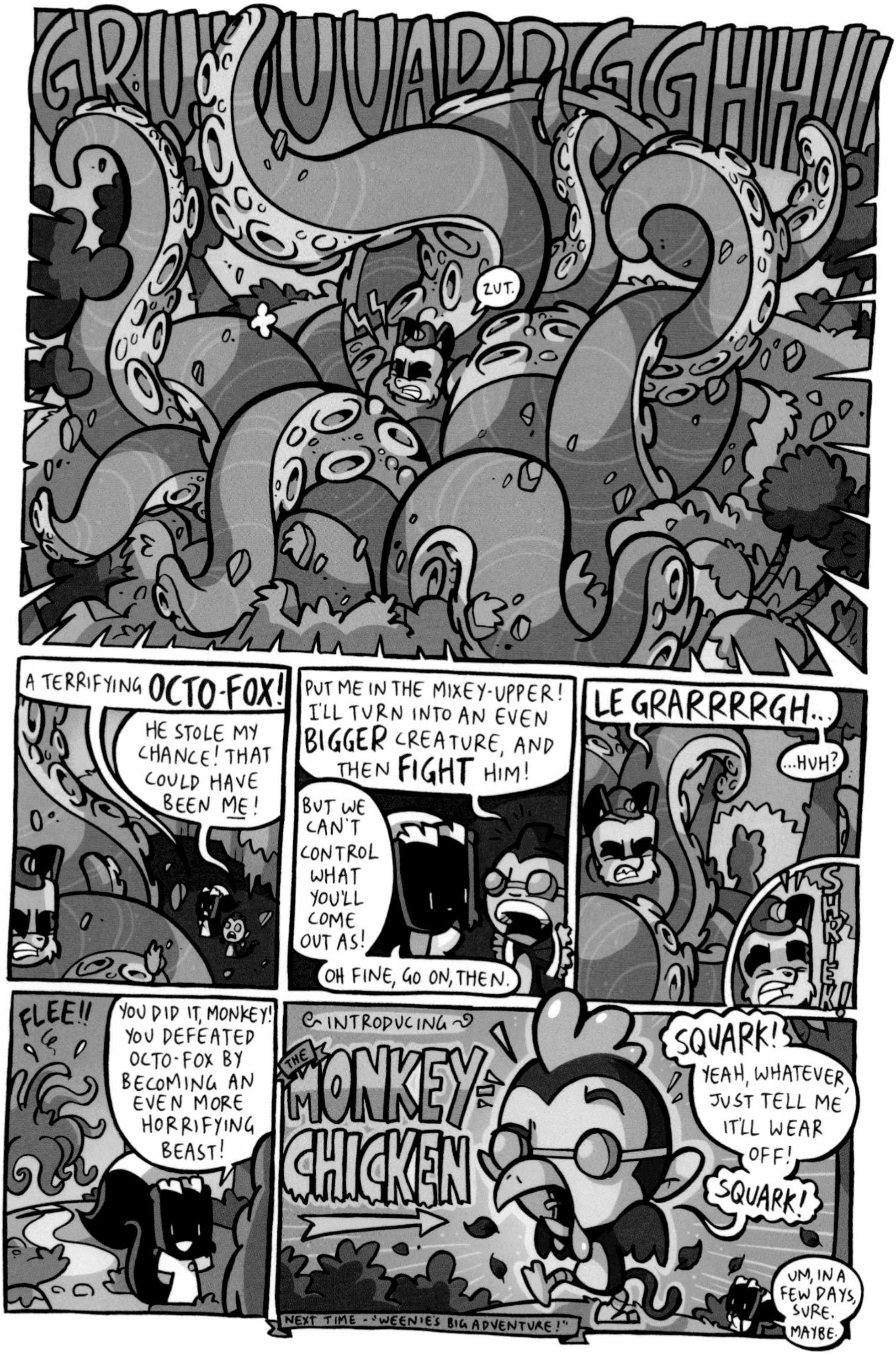
GRUUUUARRGGHH!!!
ZUT.
A TERRIFYING OCTO-FOX!
HE STOLE MY CHANCE! THAT COULD HAVE BEEN ME!
PUT ME IN THE MIXEY-UPPER! I'LL TURN INTO AN EVEN BIGGER CREATURE, AND THEN FIGHT HIM!
BUT WE CAN'T CONTROL WHAT YOU'LL COME OUT AS!
OH FINE, GO ON, THEN.
LE GRARRRRGH...
...HUH?
SHRIEK!
FLEE!!
YOU DID IT, MONKEY! YOU DEFEATED OCTO-FOX BY BECOMING AN EVEN MORE HORRIFYING BEAST!
INTRODUCING
THE MONKEY-CHICKEN
SQUARK!
YEAH, WHATEVER, JUST TELL ME IT'LL WEAR OFF!
SQUARK!
UM, IN A FEW DAYS, SURE. MAYBE.
NEXT TIME - "WEENIE'S BIG ADVENTURE!"

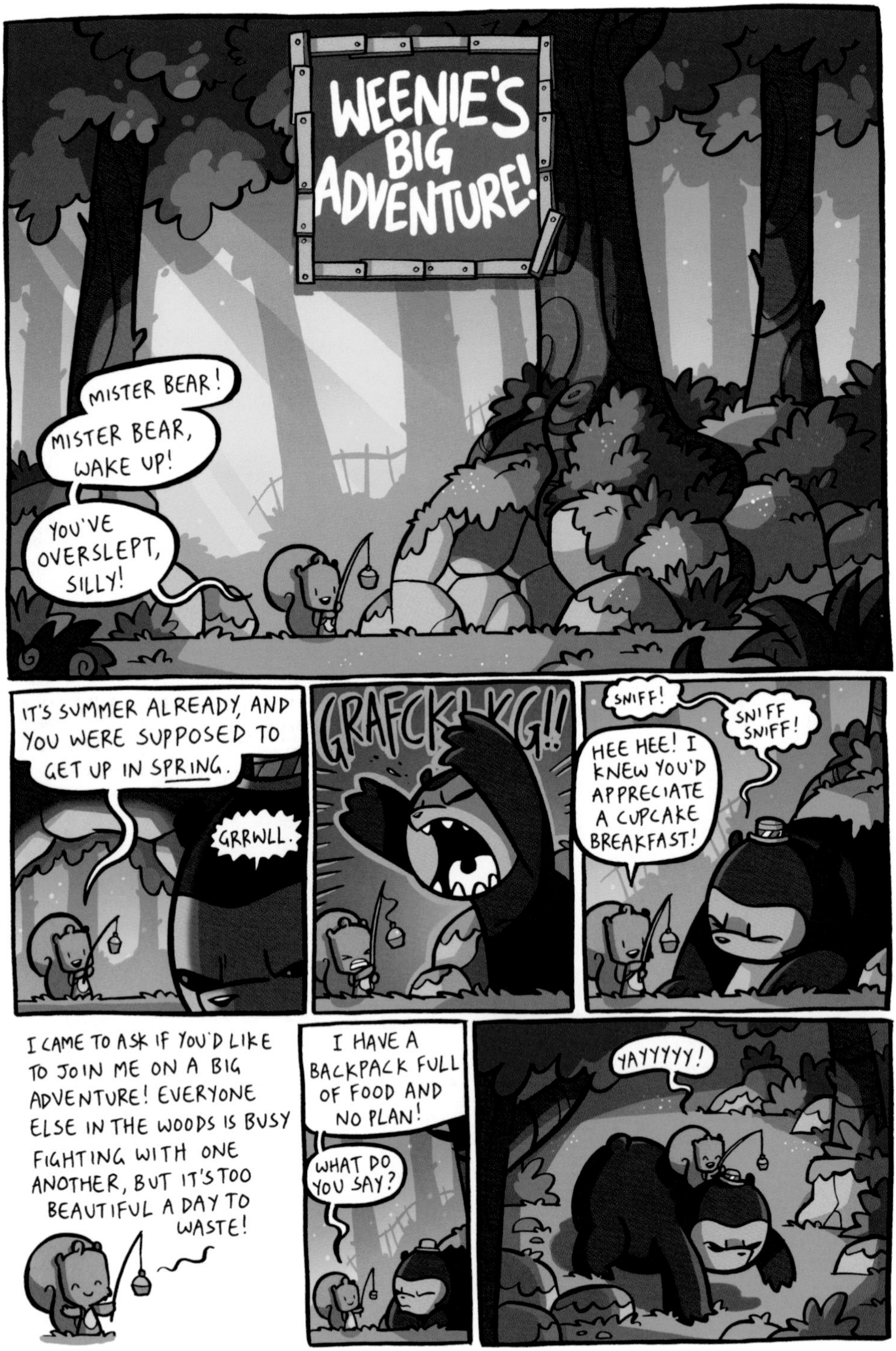
WEENIE'S BIG ADVENTURE!
MISTER BEAR!
MISTER BEAR, WAKE UP!
YOU'VE OVERSLEPT, SILLY!
IT'S SUMMER ALREADY, AND YOU WERE SUPPOSED TO GET UP IN SPRING.
GRRWLL.
GRAFCKLKG!!
SNIFF!
SNIFF SNIFF!
HEE HEE! I KNEW YOU'D APPRECIATE A CUPCAKE BREAKFAST!
I CAME TO ASK IF YOU'D LIKE TO JOIN ME ON A BIG ADVENTURE! EVERYONE ELSE IN THE WOODS IS BUSY FIGHTING WITH ONE ANOTHER, BUT IT'S TOO BEAUTIFUL A DAY TO WASTE!
I HAVE A BACKPACK FULL OF FOOD AND NO PLAN!
WHAT DO YOU SAY?
YAYYYYY!

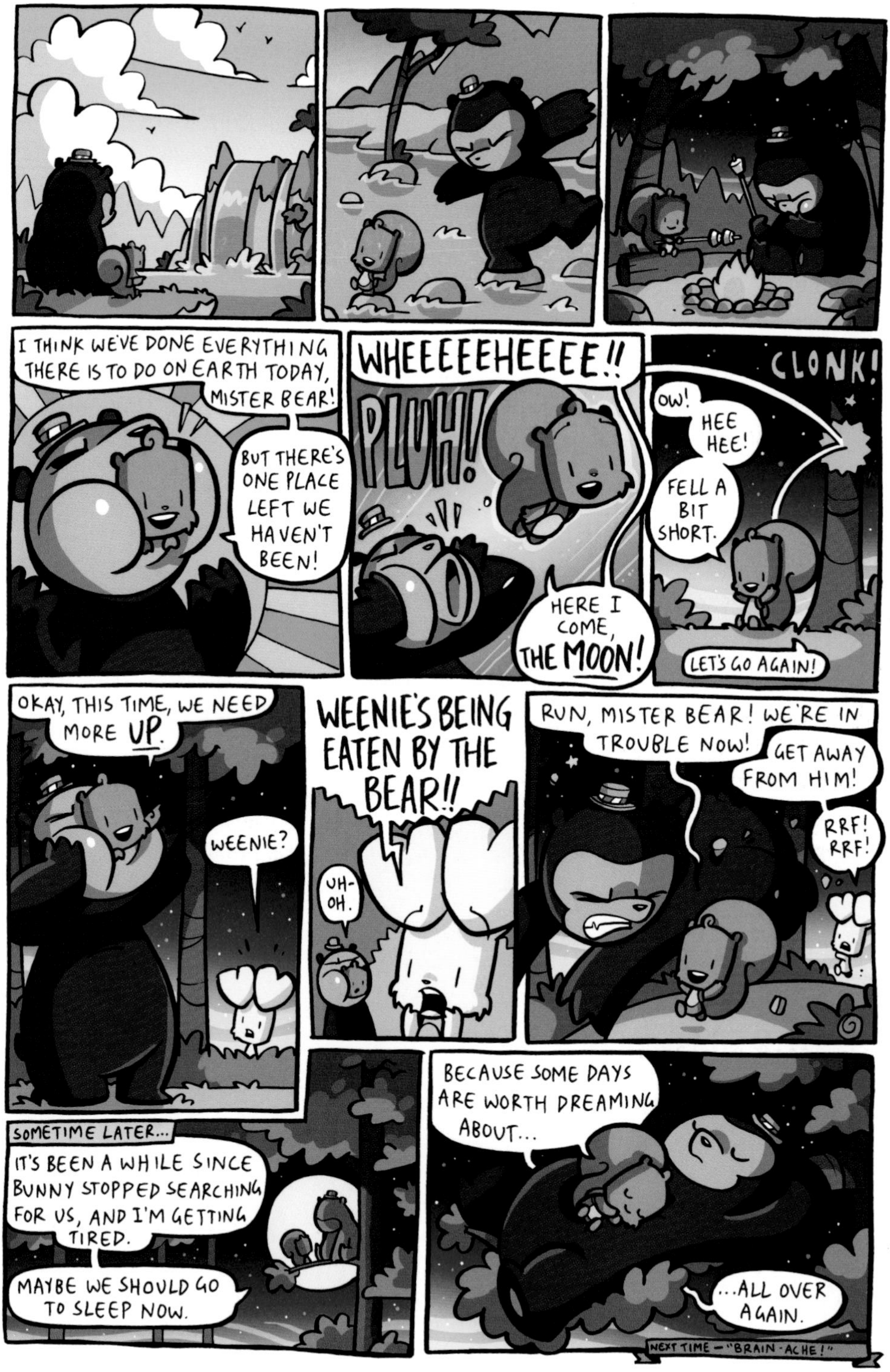
I THINK WE'VE DONE EVERYTHING THERE IS TO DO ON EARTH TODAY, MISTER BEAR!
BUT THERE'S ONE PLACE LEFT WE HAVEN'T BEEN!
WHEEEEEHEEEE!!
PLUH!
HERE I COME, THE MOON!
CLONK!
OW!
HEE HEE!
FELL A BIT SHORT.
LET'S GO AGAIN!
OKAY, THIS TIME, WE NEED MORE UP.
WEENIE?
WEENIE'S BEING EATEN BY THE BEAR!!
UH-OH.
RUN, MISTER BEAR! WE'RE IN TROUBLE NOW!
GET AWAY FROM HIM!
RRF! RRF!
SOMETIME LATER...
IT'S BEEN A WHILE SINCE BUNNY STOPPED SEARCHING FOR US, AND I'M GETTING TIRED.
MAYBE WE SHOULD GO TO SLEEP NOW.
BECAUSE SOME DAYS ARE WORTH DREAMING ABOUT...
...ALL OVER AGAIN.
NEXT TIME — "BRAIN-ACHE!"

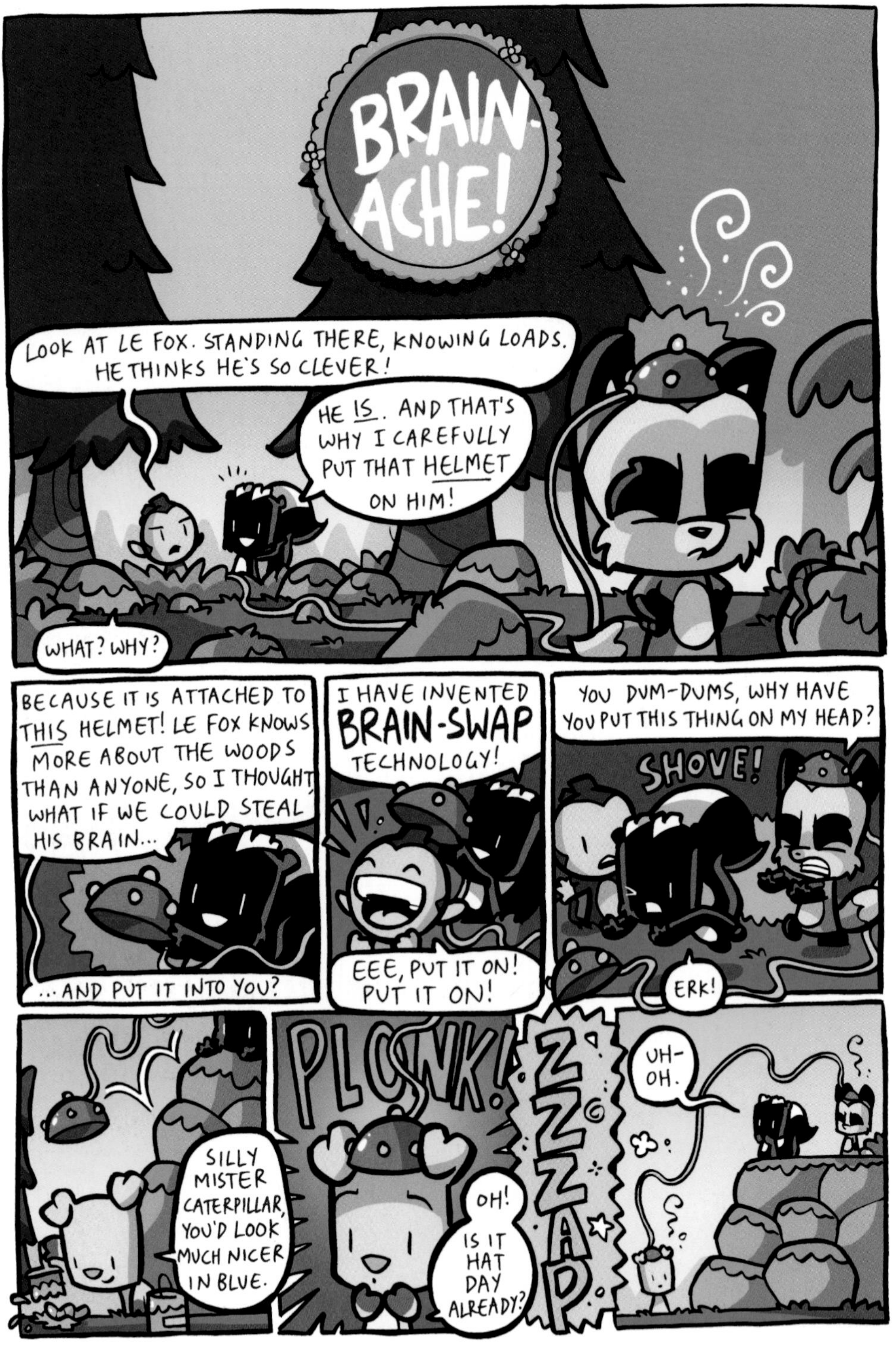
BRAIN-ACHE!
LOOK AT LE FOX. STANDING THERE, KNOWING LOADS. HE THINKS HE'S SO CLEVER!
HE IS. AND THAT'S WHY I CAREFULLY PUT THAT HELMET ON HIM!
WHAT? WHY?
BECAUSE IT IS ATTACHED TO THIS HELMET! LE FOX KNOWS MORE ABOUT THE WOODS THAN ANYONE, SO I THOUGHT, WHAT IF WE COULD STEAL HIS BRAIN...
...AND PUT IT INTO YOU?
I HAVE INVENTED BRAIN-SWAP TECHNOLOGY!
EEE, PUT IT ON! PUT IT ON!
YOU DUM-DUMS, WHY HAVE YOU PUT THIS THING ON MY HEAD?
SHOVE!
ERK!
SILLY MISTER CATERPILLAR, YOU'D LOOK MUCH NICER IN BLUE.
PLONK!
OH!
IS IT HAT DAY ALREADY?
ZZZAP
UH-OH.

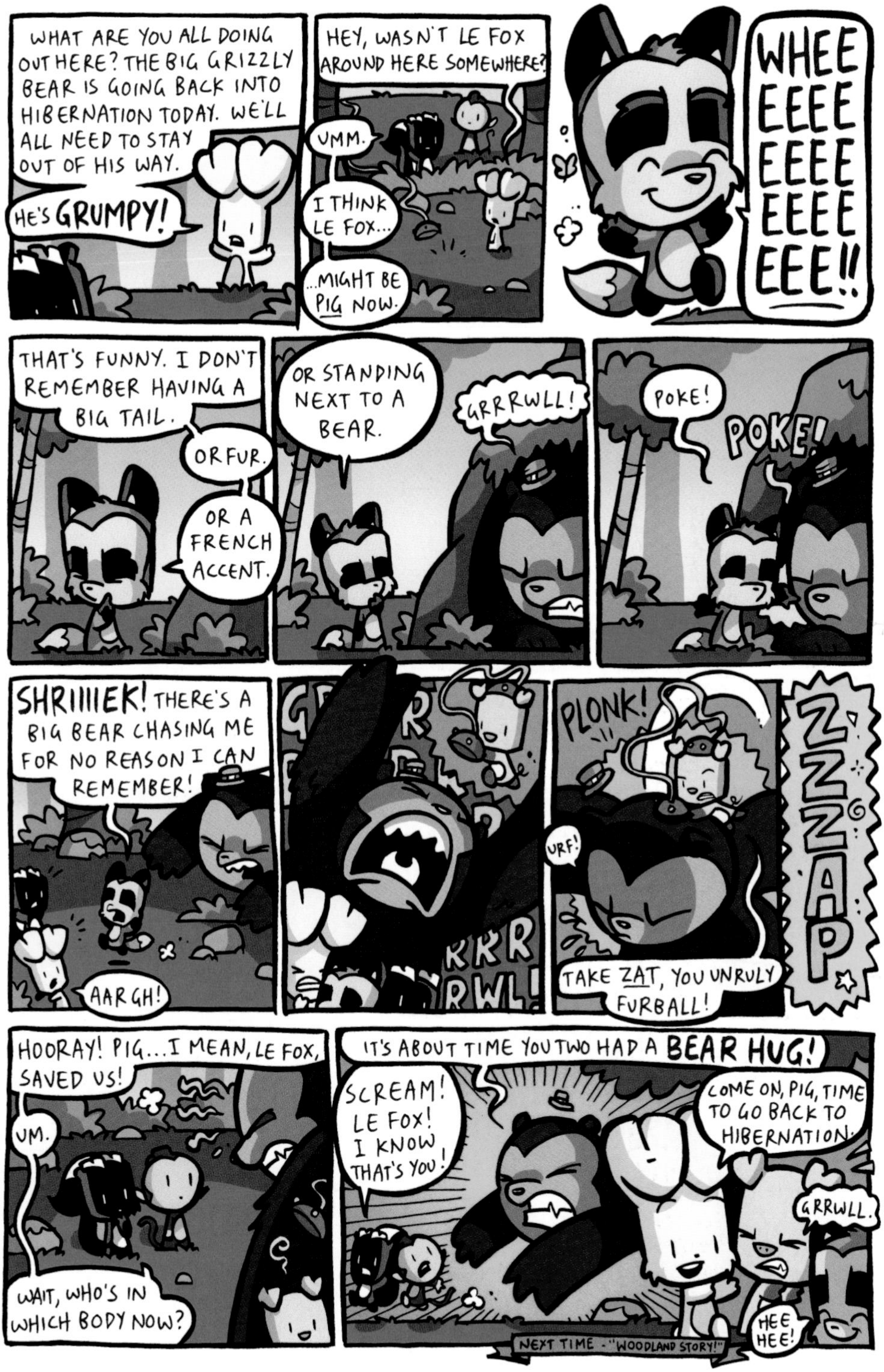
WHAT ARE YOU ALL DOING OUT HERE? THE BIG GRIZZLY BEAR IS GOING BACK INTO HIBERNATION TODAY. WE'LL ALL NEED TO STAY OUT OF HIS WAY.
HE'S GRUMPY!
HEY, WASN'T LE FOX AROUND HERE SOMEWHERE?
UMM.
I THINK LE FOX...
...MIGHT BE PIG NOW.
WHEEEEEEEEEEEEEEEEEEE!!
THAT'S FUNNY. I DON'T REMEMBER HAVING A BIG TAIL.
OR FUR.
OR A FRENCH ACCENT.
OR STANDING NEXT TO A BEAR.
GRRRWLL!
POKE!
POKE!
SHRIIIIEK! THERE'S A BIG BEAR CHASING ME FOR NO REASON I CAN REMEMBER!
AARGH!
RRR RWL!
PLONK!
URF!
TAKE ZAT, YOU UNRULY FURBALL!
ZZZAP
HOORAY! PIG...I MEAN, LE FOX, SAVED US!
UM.
WAIT, WHO'S IN WHICH BODY NOW?
IT'S ABOUT TIME YOU TWO HAD A BEAR HUG!
SCREAM! LE FOX! I KNOW THAT'S YOU!
COME ON, PIG, TIME TO GO BACK TO HIBERNATION.
GRRWLL.
HEE HEE!
NEXT TIME - "WOODLAND STORY!"

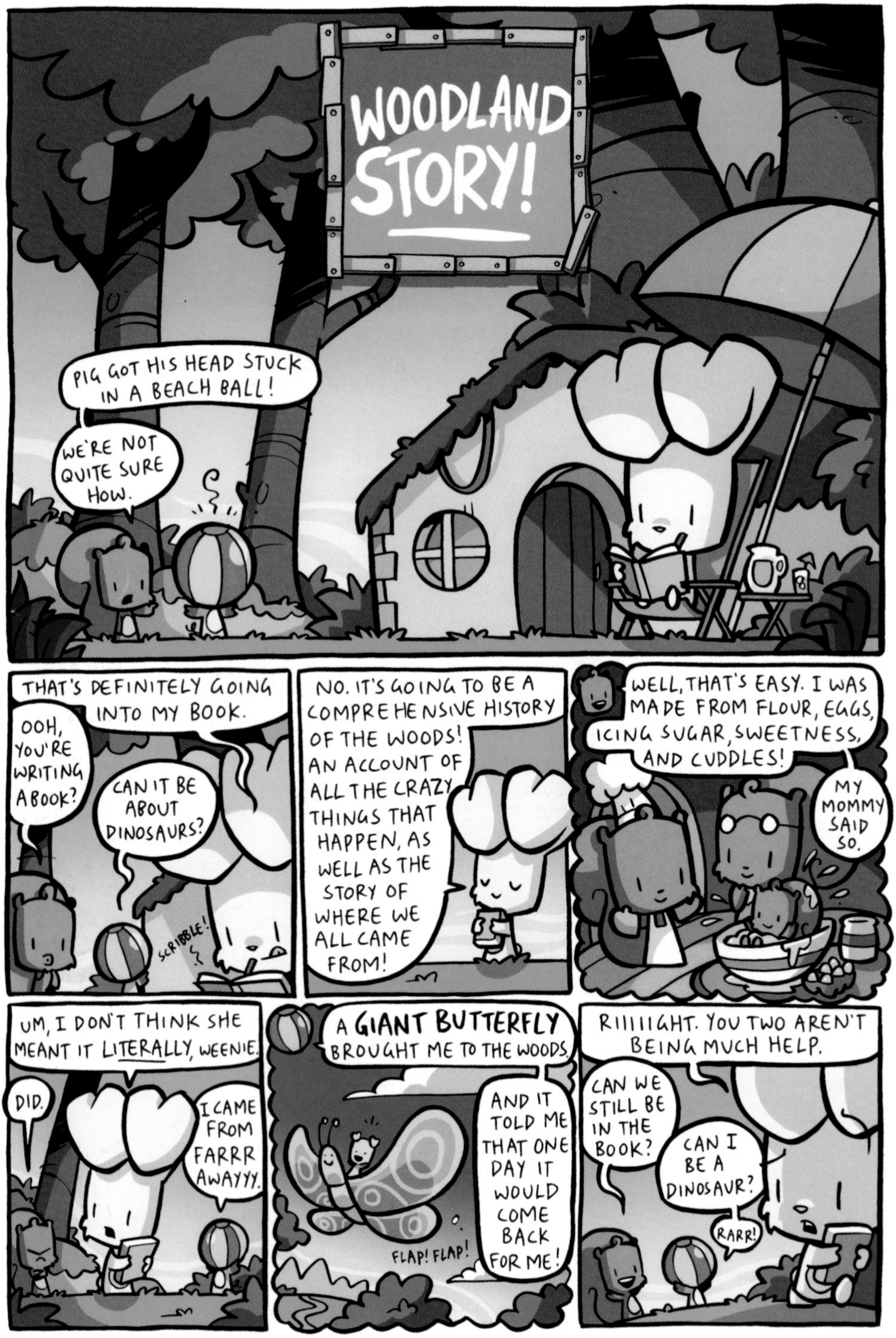

WOODLAND STORY!
PIG GOT HIS HEAD STUCK IN A BEACH BALL!
WE'RE NOT QUITE SURE HOW.
THAT'S DEFINITELY GOING INTO MY BOOK.
OOH, YOU'RE WRITING A BOOK?
CAN IT BE ABOUT DINOSAURS?
SCRIBBLE!
NO. IT'S GOING TO BE A COMPREHENSIVE HISTORY OF THE WOODS! AN ACCOUNT OF ALL THE CRAZY THINGS THAT HAPPEN, AS WELL AS THE STORY OF WHERE WE ALL CAME FROM!
WELL, THAT'S EASY. I WAS MADE FROM FLOUR, EGGS, ICING SUGAR, SWEETNESS, AND CUDDLES!
MY MOMMY SAID SO.
UM, I DON'T THINK SHE MEANT IT LITERALLY, WEENIE.
DID.
I CAME FROM FARRR AWAYYY.
A GIANT BUTTERFLY BROUGHT ME TO THE WOODS.
AND IT TOLD ME THAT ONE DAY IT WOULD COME BACK FOR ME!
FLAP! FLAP!
RIIIIIGHT. YOU TWO AREN'T BEING MUCH HELP.
CAN WE STILL BE IN THE BOOK?
CAN I BE A DINOSAUR?
RARR!

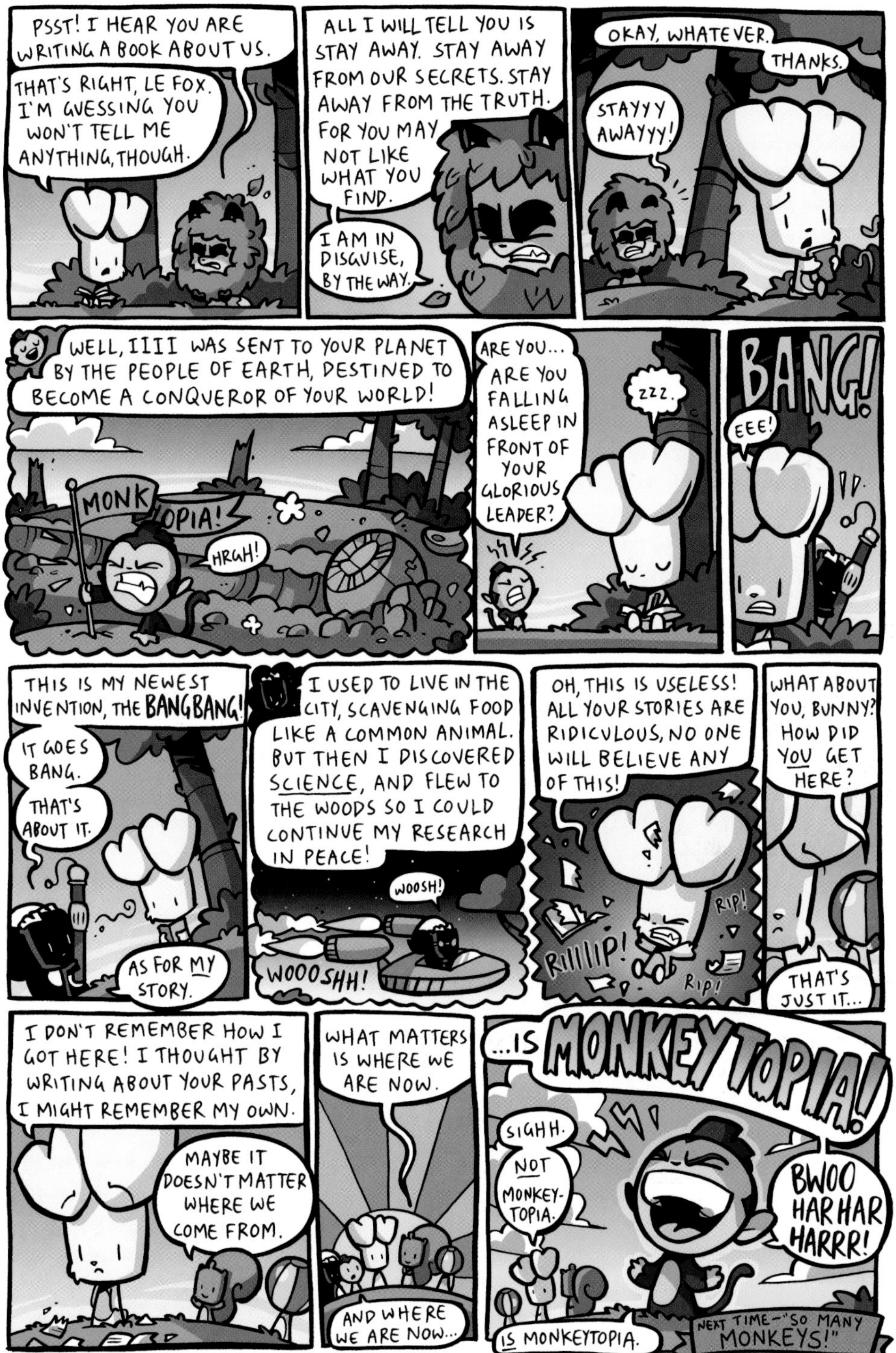
PSST! I HEAR YOU ARE WRITING A BOOK ABOUT US.
THAT'S RIGHT, LE FOX. I'M GUESSING YOU WON'T TELL ME ANYTHING, THOUGH.
ALL I WILL TELL YOU IS STAY AWAY. STAY AWAY FROM OUR SECRETS. STAY AWAY FROM THE TRUTH.
FOR YOU MAY NOT LIKE WHAT YOU FIND.
I AM IN DISGUISE, BY THE WAY.
OKAY, WHATEVER.
THANKS.
STAYYY AWAYYY!
WELL, IIII WAS SENT TO YOUR PLANET BY THE PEOPLE OF EARTH, DESTINED TO BECOME A CONQUEROR OF YOUR WORLD!
MONK
TOPIA!
HRGH!
ARE YOU...
ARE YOU FALLING ASLEEP IN FRONT OF YOUR GLORIOUS LEADER?
ZZZ.
BANG!
EEE!
THIS IS MY NEWEST INVENTION, THE BANGBANG!
IT GOES BANG.
THAT'S ABOUT IT.
AS FOR MY STORY.
I USED TO LIVE IN THE CITY, SCAVENGING FOOD LIKE A COMMON ANIMAL. BUT THEN I DISCOVERED SCIENCE, AND FLEW TO THE WOODS SO I COULD CONTINUE MY RESEARCH IN PEACE!
WOOSH!
WOOOSHH!
OH, THIS IS USELESS! ALL YOUR STORIES ARE RIDICULOUS, NO ONE WILL BELIEVE ANY OF THIS!
RIIIIIP!
RIP!
RIP!
WHAT ABOUT YOU, BUNNY? HOW DID YOU GET HERE?
THAT'S JUST IT...
I DON'T REMEMBER HOW I GOT HERE! I THOUGHT BY WRITING ABOUT YOUR PASTS, I MIGHT REMEMBER MY OWN.
MAYBE IT DOESN'T MATTER WHERE WE COME FROM.
WHAT MATTERS IS WHERE WE ARE NOW.
AND WHERE WE ARE NOW...
...IS MONKEYTOPIA!
SIGHH.
NOT MONKEY-TOPIA.
IS MONKEYTOPIA.
BWOO HAR HAR HARRR!
NEXT TIME—"SO MANY MONKEYS!"

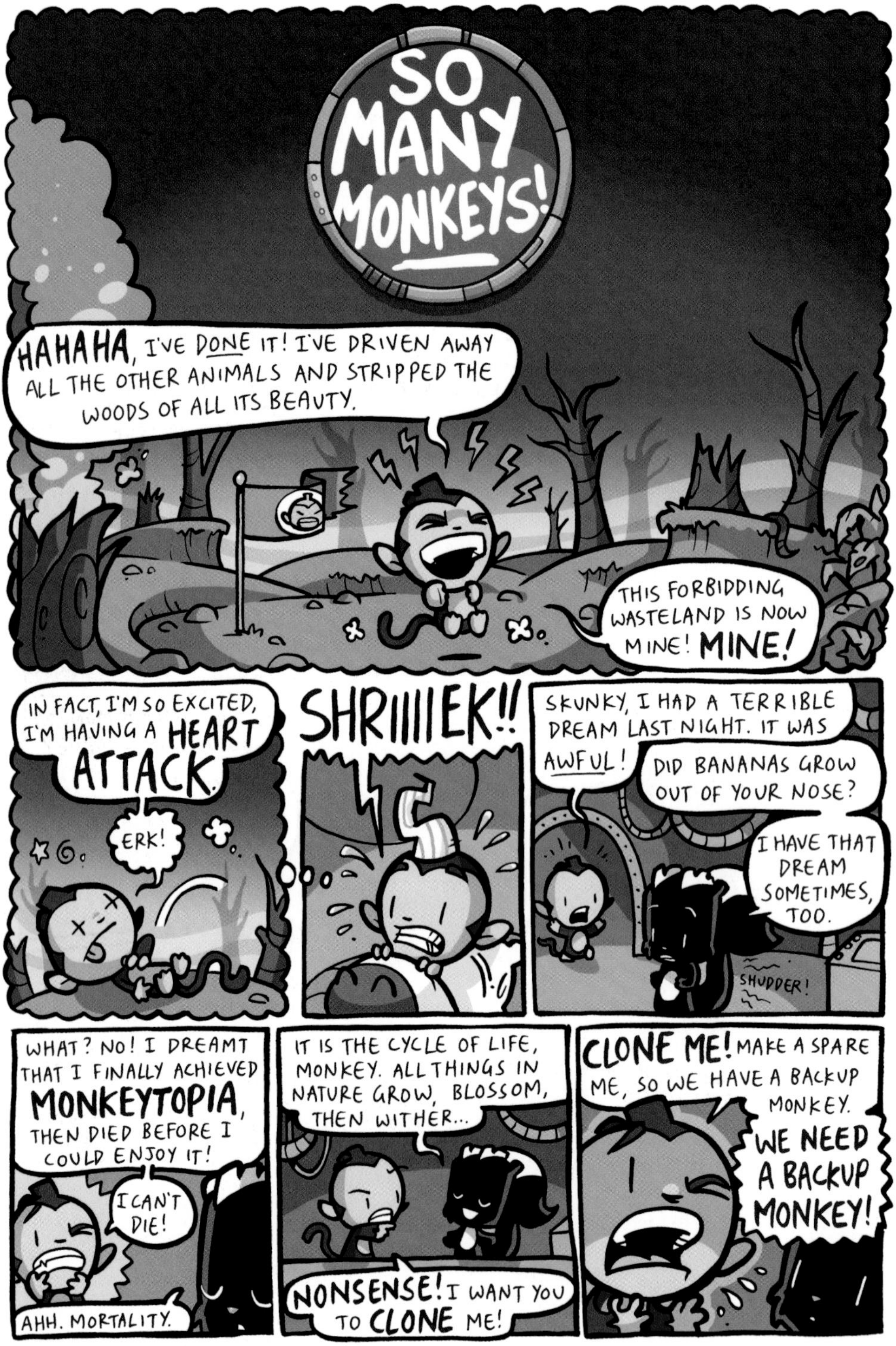
SO MANY MONKEYS!
HAHAHA, I'VE DONE IT! I'VE DRIVEN AWAY ALL THE OTHER ANIMALS AND STRIPPED THE WOODS OF ALL ITS BEAUTY.
THIS FORBIDDING WASTELAND IS NOW MINE! MINE!
IN FACT, I'M SO EXCITED, I'M HAVING A HEART ATTACK.
ERK!
SHRIIIIIEK!!
SKUNKY, I HAD A TERRIBLE DREAM LAST NIGHT. IT WAS AWFUL!
DID BANANAS GROW OUT OF YOUR NOSE?
I HAVE THAT DREAM SOMETIMES, TOO.
SHUDDER!
WHAT? NO! I DREAMT THAT I FINALLY ACHIEVED MONKEYTOPIA, THEN DIED BEFORE I COULD ENJOY IT!
I CAN'T DIE!
AHH. MORTALITY.
IT IS THE CYCLE OF LIFE, MONKEY. ALL THINGS IN NATURE GROW, BLOSSOM, THEN WITHER...
NONSENSE! I WANT YOU TO CLONE ME!
CLONE ME! MAKE A SPARE ME, SO WE HAVE A BACKUP MONKEY.
WE NEED A BACKUP MONKEY!

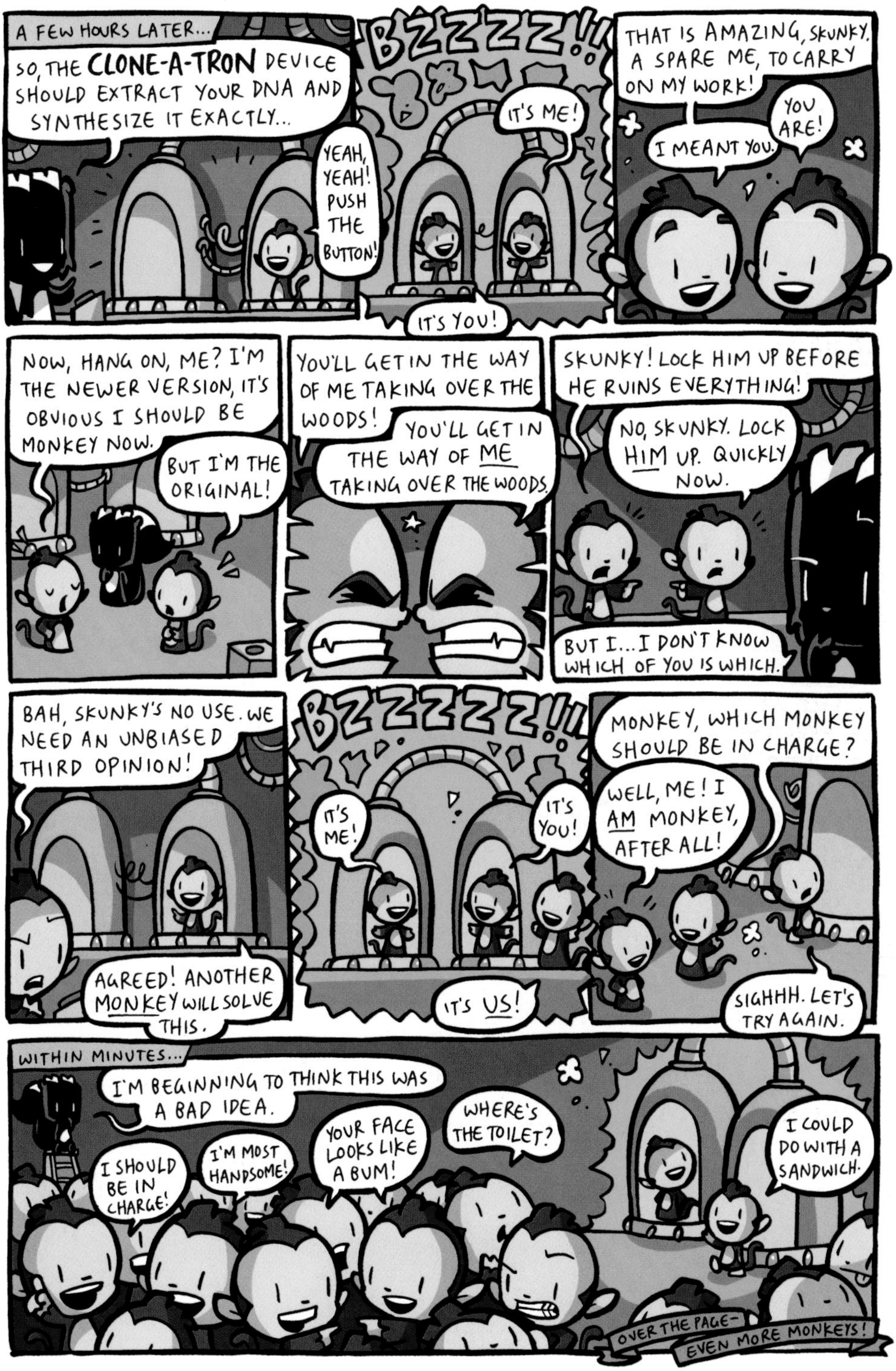
A FEW HOURS LATER...
SO, THE CLONE-A-TRON DEVICE SHOULD EXTRACT YOUR DNA AND SYNTHESIZE IT EXACTLY...
YEAH, YEAH! PUSH THE BUTTON!
BZZZZZ!!!
IT'S ME!
IT'S YOU!
THAT IS AMAZING, SKUNKY. A SPARE ME, TO CARRY ON MY WORK!
I MEANT YOU.
YOU ARE!
NOW, HANG ON, ME? I'M THE NEWER VERSION, IT'S OBVIOUS I SHOULD BE MONKEY NOW.
BUT I'M THE ORIGINAL!
YOU'LL GET IN THE WAY OF ME TAKING OVER THE WOODS!
YOU'LL GET IN THE WAY OF ME TAKING OVER THE WOODS.
SKUNKY! LOCK HIM UP BEFORE HE RUINS EVERYTHING!
NO, SKUNKY. LOCK HIM UP. QUICKLY NOW.
BUT I... I DON'T KNOW WHICH OF YOU IS WHICH.
BAH, SKUNKY'S NO USE. WE NEED AN UNBIASED THIRD OPINION!
AGREED! ANOTHER MONKEY WILL SOLVE THIS.
BZZZZZZ!!!
IT'S ME!
IT'S YOU!
IT'S US!
MONKEY, WHICH MONKEY SHOULD BE IN CHARGE?
WELL, ME! I AM MONKEY, AFTER ALL!
SIGHHH. LET'S TRY AGAIN.
WITHIN MINUTES...
I'M BEGINNING TO THINK THIS WAS A BAD IDEA.
I SHOULD BE IN CHARGE!
I'M MOST HANDSOME!
YOUR FACE LOOKS LIKE A BUM!
WHERE'S THE TOILET?
I COULD DO WITH A SANDWICH.
OVER THE PAGE— EVEN MORE MONKEYS!

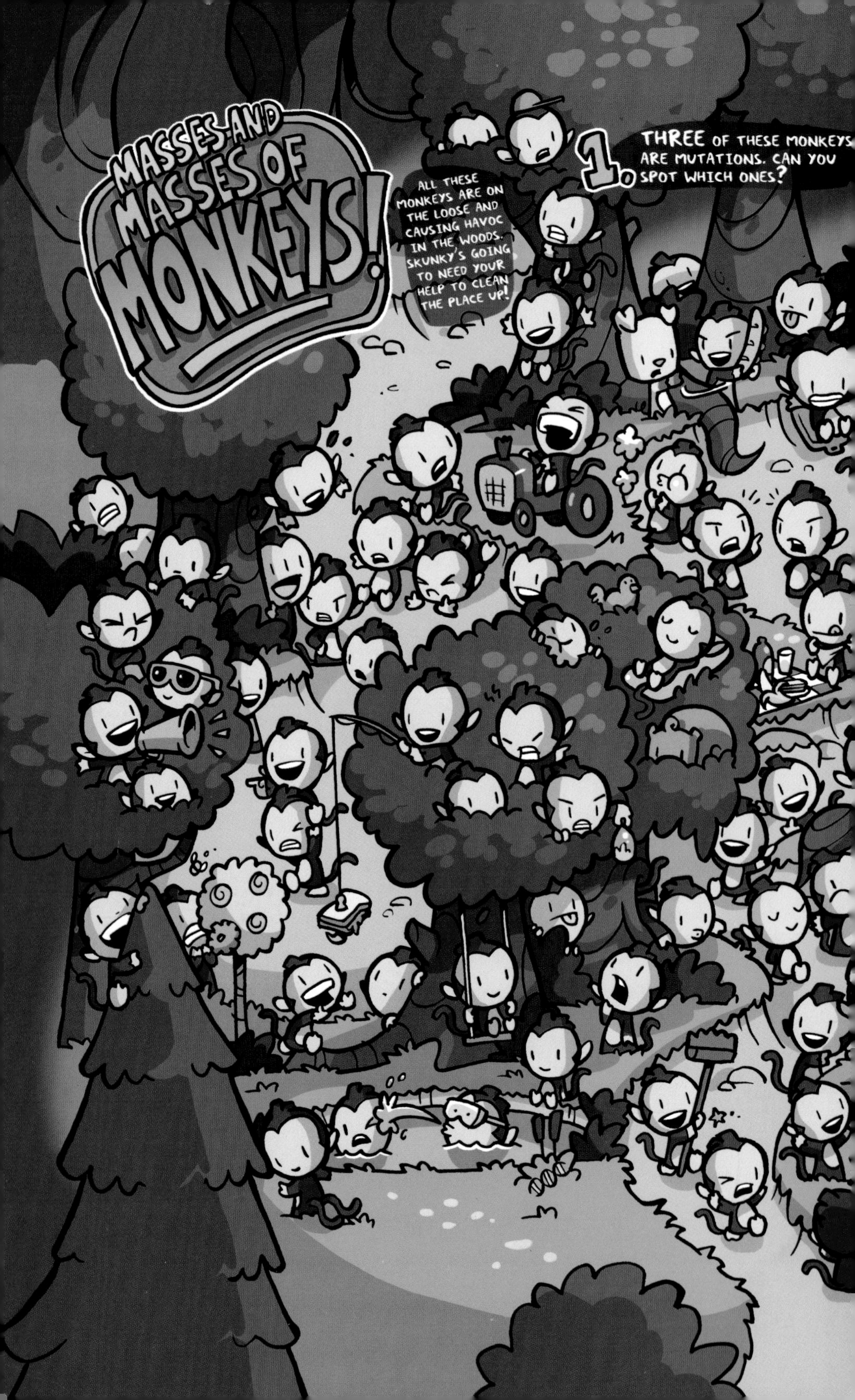
MASSES AND MASSES OF MONKEYS!
ALL THESE MONKEYS ARE ON THE LOOSE AND CAUSING HAVOC IN THE WOODS. SKUNKY'S GOING TO NEED YOUR HELP TO CLEAN THE PLACE UP!
1. THREE OF THESE MONKEYS ARE MUTATIONS. CAN YOU SPOT WHICH ONES?